# When the Beacons Blazed

## M.A. Wood

### Illustrated by
### Chris Mara

D1494241

**Byways**

**When the Beacons Blazed**

For M.G.G., who would have defended **her** tower against all comers.

First published 1983 by Byway Books
9 Maxton Court, Hawick, Roxburghshire
TD9 7QN.

©   Text M.A. Wood
©   Illustrations 1983 Byway Books

ISBN 0 907448 08 9

Phototypeset in Compugraphic English 18
and Printed in Scotland by Kelso Graphics,
The Knowes, Kelso, Roxburghshire

**This book is published witn the financial assistance of the Scottish Arts Council**

# Contents

## THE ENGLISHER

It was a lovely autumn afternoon — warm and sunny — but Christine Nancibelle Elliot, whom everybody in the little valley among the Scottish Border hills called Kirsty, looked about her with a worried frown.

The courtyard of the high square pele tower that was her home, was full of noise and activity as men moved like so many busy ants between the numerous out-buildings round the foot of the tower. Some were bringing out horses from the stable and leading them across to Wullie Smith's forge to have their shoes changed from front to back in order that the hoof prints would thus baffle any pursuers. Others were laughing and jostling as they tried to be first to sharpen their swords and spears at the great grindstone.

Several more were standing at the door of the lean-to which served as a kitchen, trying to coax the servant girls to supply them with oaten bannocks to carry in their pouches for the journey, and in yet another corner a quieter group sitting on the edge of a large stone watering trough were checking over their arrows and testing their bow-strings.

As she watched the scene Kirsty's big green eyes grew more and more troubled, and she gave a little sigh. There was going to be a raid that night, her father's men were going on a foray into England — and Kirsty did NOT like raids!

People could be killed on raids and whenever Kirsty saw the troop riding out she got a cold niggly frightened feeling that something might happen which would shatter the security of her little home world for ever.

Of course she knew there had to be raids — everybody said so — for how else could they live through the long hard winter if they didn't take plenty of cattle from the proud English, who had pastures full of lush grass to fatten many more, while the Scots had only woods and bogs, and poor stony fields painfully hewn out of the hillsides, to grow their meagre crops.

But that didn't stop Kirsty remembering an experience she'd had when she was very small. She'd been in a naughty mood that long ago night and instead of going quietly off to sleep when Elspeth, her nurse, had put her to bed in the room at the top of the tower, Kirsty had only closed her eyes and lain still till she heard the pounding of hoofs as the men cantered up the hill to the tower after a raid. Then she'd got up again and pattered down the twisting stone staircase to see them.

She could almost feel the cold snow as she recalled dancing excitedly from one bare foot to the other, while the main gate to the courtyard swung slowly open. As the first horse appeared she'd dashed to the mounting block where everyone would be sure to see her, intending to call a merry greeting to her father and then to each of the men-at-arms who petted and played with her whenever they had time to spare.

In they clattered. She was just opening her mouth to shout when she saw the awful thing and her welcoming cry changed to a scream of terror.

The rider immediately behind her father carried another man hanging limply over the front of his horse. It was Robbie, her current favourite, who only that morning had galloped round the courtyard with Kirsty perched laughing on his shoulders.

His ruddy face was a ghastly shade of white, his mouth was half open in an animal-like snarl with a smudge of red at one side, and his glassy eyes stared unseeingly at the October moon.

Kirsty hardly knew what happened next. Her father snatched her, still crying hysterically, from the mounting block and handed her to Elspeth who had come down the stairs behind her.

For the next few days she was kept in their room at the top of the tower, as a punishment Elspeth said. Afterwards everything went back to normal except that Robbie had disappeared. Nobody mentioned him, but the other men played with Kirsty oftener than usual and Elspeth occasionally let her have honey on her porridge which was a great treat.

But ... soon the dreadful dreams began. Pictures of wildly galloping horses, flaring torches and people with pale unnatural faces kept swirling through her mind till she woke up sobbing that Robbie was dead and she'd never see him again.

It must have gone on a long time for she could remember thinking the days were lengthening out at last, the evening her father, Big Wat Elliot, took her on his knee and explained everything.

Robbie, he said, wasn't dead at all. He had merely gone to heaven to be with the Blessed Virgin and Kirsty's own mother, who was there already, and would be telling them what a good, clever, little lass Kirsty was growing into — and Kirsty must be brave and not worry about raids any more. People were very seldom injured seriously and besides, as everybody knew, one Scot could always beat two English.

'But they hurt you, didn't they?' she'd asked, gently fingering the long scar which ran down one side of Big Wat's rough, weather-beaten face,

'Och! Hoots! That was just when I was too young to know how to hold my sword properly.' he replied.

Kirsty had felt comforted after that and the nightmares had gradually ceased, but now she was a big girl, nearly ten, she realised that what her father said had not been strictly true. He had only been trying to be kind. Though none of their own men had ever died from a raid again, they often came home with wounds and gashes, but Elspeth kept a good supply of herbs for doctoring and after a few days of poulticing and bandaging they were as well as ever. Elspeth sometimes let Kirsty watch and she found it most interesting.

'Noo then, Mistress Kirsty, dinna stand day-dreaming!' the voice of old Andrew, her father's steward and right-hand man, broke into her thoughts. He was leading two of the small, wiry horses the Borderers used.

'You're blocking the track. I've just seen young Sim an' he said to tell you he was just off to the Lynn Pool for a bit fishing an' would you no like to gang along?'

'Oh, I would! Oh, thank you, Andrew!' Kirsty forgot her troubles immediately. She loved being with Sim, a sturdy red-haired boy, slightly older than herself. They generally managed to have some adventures, though as Kirsty ran off to ask Elspeth's permission for the outing, she never guessed that the one ahead was going to be the biggest yet — was going to change her life in fact.

Sim was the only one of the local children she was allowed to play with. They had been friends for the past two years since Sim had won Elspeth's favour by snatching Kirsty out of the path of a wildly charging stirk (bullock), soon after he'd come to the village beside the tower.

Before that Sim had lived far out among the hills where his father was a ranger, hunting the wild deer for a livelihood, until he had the misfortune to meet an angry stag which gored him so badly he later died of the wound. Afterwards Sim's mother brought her children to Biglynn Glen to be near their uncle who was one of Big Wat's followers. So Sim had to work hard to help support his

10

small brothers and sisters, usually by herding cattle.

'I'll get a piece for you both to eat at the Pool,' said Elspeth when she heard what was afoot and with Kirsty dancing along beside her, went to the spence (larder) where she filled the little girl's own basket with slices of rye bread and hunks of tasty ewe's milk cheese.

Then, hardly listening to Elspeth's reminder not to get into mischief and to be home well before dark, Kirsty raced off as fast as she could go.

She caught up with Sim just where their little valley narrowed to the waterfall which gave the place its name, and when she called to the boy he stopped and waited for her.

'Oh, I'm so glad Andrew gave you the message,' he said with a broad smile on his freckled face, 'I darna come inside in case I got saddled with any jobs. 'Tis such a braw day I wanted to make the most of it. It might weel be the last free time I'll have if they fetch plenty of cattle back tonight. Oh, how I wish I was going with them! It must be wonderful riding over the hills in the moonlight...'

'Oh Sim, don't!' begged Kirsty.

'What a goose you are about raids,' said

the boy, 'and the Laird the bravest reiver (raider) this side the Border — except Nebless Nick,' he added, 'and My Lord Maxwell of course.'

Kirsty shivered, The great Lord Maxwell, Warden of the Western Border Marches and next in importance to the king himself, was just a name to her, but Nebless Nick, a cruel ruthless raider who lived in the neighbouring valley was very real indeed. He hated the English — and most other people — because his face had been disfigured by a sword cut. Her father and Elspeth had always tried to protect Kirsty from learning too much about the savage things which were sometimes done on the Border but she'd managed to hear about some of them, and Nebless Nick was often involved. There was a story of him putting out a prisoner's eyes which made her cover her ears and run away.

Unfortunately he considered himself Big Wat's immediate superior and occasionally visited Biglynn Tower. Kirsty hated these times when her usually happy home became gloomy and silent. She always stayed upstairs with Elspeth and watched his coming and going from the topmost window. It was the nearest to Nebless Nick she ever wanted to be!

I wouldn't like you to get hurt,' she said now in reply to Sim's previous remarks.

'Och, havers! Who's feart o' a dunt or twa?' retorted Sim stoutly, 'Why last week I fought Tom and … and …' he named several of the biggest village boys, 'You should have seen Tom's black eye.' Then observing Kirsty's look of disgust, hastily changed the subject, 'Besides aren't you always saying I'm to be your knight and win your favour in the lists?'

Kirsty had never seen a tournament, but once when he'd been at the King's court in distant Edinburgh, Big Wat had attended one and Kirsty never tired of hearing about the colour, and the Pageantry, and the richly dressed ladies headed by the Queen of Beauty who awarded the victor with a chaplet of laurel.

In spite of Elspeth's disapproving remarks about girls who ran and climbed like boys, Kirsty was quite sure that she too would be Queen of Beauty some day, and, of course, Sim who good naturedly went along with her imaginings as he always did, would be her knight.

But there would be no need for him to prove his valour today. Kirsty resolutely put all thoughts of fighting out of her mind. It was too lovely an afternoon for that, they were just going to have a nice, peaceful time by the Biglynn Burn without any grown-ups to bother them.

The children had now reached the waterfall, and paused as always, to gaze down at the deep, dark pool at its foot, before doing anything else. It was a dangerous place, and before they had come there first, Big Wat had warned Sim most severely never to attempt to swim in it till he was grown to man's full strength, and NEVER, NEVER allow Kirsty to try to do so.

But there was a tree-shaded bit lower down the stream where they like to fish, and afterwards ate their food and dozed awhile with the sound of the water lulling them to sleep.

When Kirsty opened her eyes again the sun had shifted slightly but there was still plenty of time before they needed to return home. She felt restless now and decided on one of her favourite games of make-belief which she only played when they were at the waterfall.

Running a few yards upstream, she scrambled over the rocks beside the pool and climbed to the top of a particularly large boulder.

'I'm the spirit of the pool!' she announced as she stood poised with her arms outstretched and her long dark hair flowing behind her, 'I shall grant you three wishes, mortal. What'll they be?'

Sim who had followed her slowly, sat down lazily at the foot of the boulder and laughed up at her. 'You'll get a surprise if the real spirits o' the pool hear you,' he teased. 'What if the water demon reaches out his arms and pulls you in?'

'He won't — they won't mind. They know it's only fun,' said Kirsty confidently, 'besides I gave them some cheese from my piece to make sure, didn't you see me? So come on — tell me your wishes ... oh, what's that?'

The noise of trampling hooves and harsh shouts suddenly mingled with the sound of the waterfall. For a wild minute she thought Sim's jest had come true. Were the demons of the lynn about to attack them?

Then springing hastily from her perch she saw it was only a small party of mounted men picking their way down the rugged hillside. Their shouts echoing across the glen made them sound more numerous than they were.

As the children watched, some of the riders positioned themselves on the slopes around the waterfall while three others came straight towards the side of the pool. It was then the leader noticed the children and drew up his great bay horse just beside Kirsty. He glared down at her from under the rim of his steel cap and Kirsty stared back in horror. She was seeing Nebless Nick face to face at last — and what a face!

'Noo, wha've we here? Wha's bairn art ye, lass?' he asked in a loud, rasping voice which matched his looks.

Kirsty tried to curtsy as Elspeth had carefully taught her, but it is difficult to be graceful when your heart is thumping madly and you are standing on rough ground with bare feet.

'If — if you please, sir — my lord,' she stammered, 'I'm Kirsty Elliot of Biglynn Tower.'

'H'm, Big Wat's daughter, eh?' said Nebless Nick giving what would have been a smile in anybody else, 'an' a weel grown bit lass too. Strange I havena seen ye afore. I'd thought ye were still in leading strings.'

Kirsty felt rather annoyed. Only babies wore leading strings — when they were learning to walk!

'An' yon'll be your sweetheart ne doot,' Nebless Nick leered in Sim's direction, and went on, 'What'd ye say to coming to dwell in my place in a few years time? My lady wife would like fine to have such a bonny maid to sort her 'broidery threads an' help her make some of these new fashioned tapestries she's so set on, for our hall.'

Kirsty was crosser than ever. She knew well-born girls generally went from home to be waiting maids to some great lady, but fancy thinking she would leave her father, Elspeth, Sim and everybody she cared about, to go and work for Nebless Nick's grim-faced wife — who was said to be as cruel as himself — and sew her horrid tapestries. Kirsty didn't like her needle at the best of times and only tolerated the daily task Elspeth insisted on, because her nurse told the strange old Border legends about witches and fairies while they worked. Kirsty was sure no one could possibly play or tell stories in Nebless Nick's home — but what did one say to one's overlord?

'I — I thank you,' she faltered, 'but I — I don't think my father would let me. He — he likes me to pour out his wine in the evenings.'

'Ha, ye can pour mine instead. I'll speak till him aboot it. But noo, stand back a minute, bairns, an' ye'll see a big splash!'

As he spoke he signed to the men behind him. One dismounted and lowered a long bundle which he'd been carrying before him, to the ground. The other man also

jumped from his horse and bent to pick up one end of the bundle.

Together they advanced to the pool swinging the bundle gently as they prepared to toss it into the water, and at that moment Kirsty realized their burden was a curly haired boy, tightly tied in a dark green riding cloak.

He looked as if he might be older than the children, but his blue eyes were dazed with fear and his pale terrified face reminded Kirsty of her old nightmares about Robbie. And they were going to throw him into the pool!

'OH DON'T!' screamed Kirsty, 'Oh, don't drown him! Please — please! He's only a boy!'

Impulsively she stepped towards Nebless Nick and clasped his iron shod foot. It was as high as she could reach.

'Tush, what ails ye, lass! He's just a bit English scum.'

'Oh, you're cruel! You mustn't! It's wrong! My father'd never kill a prisoner.'

'Nay, Because he's lily-livered, that's what! Everybody in the Western Marches kens Big Wat's a great softie!'

This was too much. Kirsty's temper got the better of her discretion.

'He's NOT! How dare you say so!' she

19

stamped her foot with rage and hit a stone which made her angrier still. 'It's a wicked lie — you know it is! We'll have you at deadly feud for that!'

This was the worst possible thing a Borderer could say and meant their families must keep on fighting for generations till there was nobody left to slay. Kirsty was so furious she didn't care, but Nebless Nick merely laughed as if she'd said something amusing.

'Noo, ye're speaking like a proper reiver's bairn!' he roared, 'Deadly feud! HA! HA! Ye've pluck after all. I never thought it. Why, I've half a mind to give ye the prisoner for that. His ransom'd make a fine dowery for when ye get married. What'd ye pay for him?'

'Oh, anything! Anything!' promised Kirsty extravagantly. Her temper was cooling. She didn't understand what he was talking about for no-one had explained with a dowery girls could be married for their money. But she knew there was a bag of gold coins in the chest beside Big Wat's bed and he'd be sure to give her enough to buy the prisoner. Kirsty was used to getting her own way — especially after she'd pestered a while.

'What aboot a kiss then?' demanded

Nebless Nick bending towards her. His foul, hot breath touched her face and before she could stop herself, Kirsty winced. It was a fatal move. Nebless Nick's mood changed at once.

'Come on get back, bairns! We've had enough play-acting. There's some men's work noo.'

Kirsty pulled herself together and would have begun pleading again but Sim grasped her arm and she felt him give it a little squeeze.

'Come away, Mistress Kirsty,' he said, 'dinna fash yourself for an Englisher.'

She turned and saw his left eyelid flicker in a warning wink. Obediently she moved away from Nebless Nick's horse and at that very moment there was a commotion behind them. Looking round quickly she saw the horse belonging to the man who'd carried the prisoner, rearing up and jerking its reins free of the bush it was tied to. Then it dashed madly down the valley. The man tried to run after it but was hampered by his mailed boots. The other trooper jumped on his own horse and made off in pursuit, with the first man leaping on behind him as he passed. At the same time those who'd been watching from a distance joined in the chase too. Horses were the most valuable things the Borderers had and they couldn't afford to loose any.

Almost instantly Nebless Nick's mount bolted as well. Sim grabbed Kirsty drawing her out of the way with such energy both children fell to the ground and rolled down the incline away from the stream.

As they struggled to their feet, bruised and breathless, Sim was chuckling.

'THAT DID IT!' he cried gleefully, 'Quick, Kirsty, let's get him loosed and see what we've found. They'll be back any minute.'

The horsemen were now mere dots in the distance, and the prisoner was lying quite still with his eyes closed. He didn't even look up when the children approached.

Kirsty clutched Sim's hand. 'Is — is he ...? she whispered.

'Dead? Not him!' Sim contemptuously poked the boy with his foot, 'Huh! Fancy fainting when you're being rescued! My father aye said the English were feckless. Bring some water from the burn to fetch him round — and hurry, Kirsty! We must get away. I'll be having a thrashing for this job — and I'd rather the Laird did it than Nebless Nick.' As he spoke Sim was busily cutting the ropes binding the captive.

Kirsty had nothing to carry water in but

she cupped her hands and managed to get enough to pour on the boy's face. With relief she saw him open his eyes, give a strong shudder and try to raise himself.

'Oh,' he said making a feeble attempt to smile, 'I thought those ruffians were drowning me! But **you** saved me, ma'am — my lady.'

Kirsty felt flattered. It was the first time anyone had addressed her with such formality.

'Oh no, **I** didn't do anything,' she said in what she believed to be a gracious, fine lady manner, ''It was Sim who made the horses bolt. He pricked them with his knife!'

'Sim? Oh, your servant? But it was you who pleaded for me — like one of the Blessed Saints themselves. Surely you must be a noble gentlewoman?'

'She's the Laird's daughter — and I'm not a servant!' interrupted Sim huffily, 'I'm the Laird's man and hers too. They call me Simon — Simon's Sim. What's **your** name?'

'Francis — Francis Milverton.' The boy was sitting up now, and he spoke so strangely they could hardly understand him. 'Where am I? This must be Scotland I suppose?'

'Oh yes,' said Kirsty, 'this is all our valley — Biglynn Glen. Isn't it lovely? My home's the Tower away down there ... But —' she suddenly remembered the danger they were in, 'we'll have to hide before Nebless Nick comes back — can you walk?'

'Of course he can.' Sim began hauling the slightly built English boy to his feet. 'Take his arm on the other side, Kirsty. We'll go to the cave.'

'Oh yes.' agreed Kirsty thankfully. She couldn't stand another encounter with Nebless Nick.

So with Francis stumbling along between them — his legs were still stiff from being tied up — the children made their way to the hollow among the rocks which Sim had referred to as the cave.

When they were comfortably huddled together in the small space the stranger told them more about himself.

'I'm staying at Naworth Castle in Cumberland, with my uncle who is one of Lord Dacre's gentlemen. You see, my father thought I was too spoilt at home and if I were to see some fighting up here it would prepare me for the proper wars on the Continent. I'm joining my father's old regiment later of course.'

'But if you were in England however did Nebless Nick get hold of you?' Sim wanted to know.

'You mean that villain? Oh, is that what you call him? Well it was really my own fault,' the boy confessed rather shamefacedly, 'It's been so boring since I came and the morning was so bright I thought I'd go for a ride by myself — then when I came to a place where the river seemed fordable I crossed it — Uncle had told me the opposite bank was Scotland — and before I'd gone very far those men just came out of nowhere and grabbed me... Ooh! it was TERRIBLE! That creature's face! I've never seen anything like it. He held a dagger to my throat — then he said I wasn't worth wasting steel on and he'd drown me like a kitling — what is a kitling?'

'A kitten!' said Sim scornfully.

'Oh!' Francis turned red. Kirsty felt sorry for him. Sim needn't always be so rude she thought.

'But why did you want to come to Scotland?' she asked quickly, 'when you were safe at home?'

'It's been so dull. The other boys at Naworth are older than me — and I thought there'd be raids and fighting all the time — and I did so want to tell my sisters in my next letter that I'd been in Scotland.'

'That was daft!' commented Sim, and Kirsty, forgetting everything else in this new interest said: 'You've got sisters? I wish I had. Do tell us all about them.'

So Francis did, and Kirsty listened eagerly, not always quite understanding everything, but ashamed of showing her ignorance by asking too many questions.

It was like some strange new fairy-tale. Isabelle, the eldest of the family was up in London attending a lady of the court and enjoying what Francis called 'balls and banquets.' They were all very proud of her because she had danced with the King and he had actually said how graceful she was.

Katherine, the next in age after himself, was a home loving bookworm, happily studying Latin and Greek — what on earth could they be, wondered Kirsty — and working in the still-room. She was also exceedingly good at sewing and was helping their mother embroider hangings for the best bed. Ugh! Poor thing! Kirsty was thinking, remembering Nebless Nick's suggestion of similar employment. When Francis, who was fumbling in his jerkin said, 'Wait — look here ... Oh, I hope I haven't lost it ... No, here 'tis. She made this as a parting gift.'

He held out a small embroidered purse decorated with an elaborate pattern of interwoven leaves and flowers, all worked in gold and coloured threads. Kirsty stared in amazement. It was the most exquisite thing she had ever seen — and done by another child! What a blessing Elspeth wasn't there to see it too!

At least Francis' other sister seemed to be ordinary. Clarissa, he said was a merry little romp of about Kirsty's own age, who escaped from her lessons with the family chaplin whenever she could.

He was going on to recount some of Clarissa's mischievous pranks, when Sim who had been listening in glum silence, suddenly said: 'It's coming on dark. We'd best be awa' hame.'

'Mercy! So it is.' Kirsty sprang to her feet. 'Are you all right, Francis? What'll you do now?'

He got up too and stretched. 'I'm fine — but rather, er — empty. What's my quickest way home?'

'England's **miles** away — over the hills. You can't go alone,' replied Kirsty, 'You'd get lost or — or — fall in a bog or something.'

'But I **must** go.' Francis turned to Sim, 'Couldn't you guide me? Or aren't there any other people nearby who could? I've money — I can pay.'

'No.' said Sim shortly, 'The folk here-abouts would kill you for your braw doublet, never mind the siller in yon fancy pouch. An' I couldna take you if I would. I dinna ken the tracks — I won't till I'm old enough to ride a foray with the men.'

Francis looked at him with rather startled expression.

'You mean you're going to be a **robber** when you're grown-up?'

'Not a robber!' retorted Sim, 'Borderers dinna steal. We're REIVERS!'

'Oh!' said Francis somewhat doubtfully, and returned to his original question. 'Well, what shall I do if you really won't help me?'

'I've told ye I canna. An' I wouldn't either.' said Sim. 'I've done enough for you the day. D'ye think I'm looking forward to the leathering I'll get?'

'Oh, don't quarrel.' Kirsty was thinking frantically. They had rescued Francis but what were they going to do with him now? And she had never seen Sim so surly before — in another minute the boys might be fighting. 'Oh, I know!' she cried in relief as inspiration struck her, 'He can come home with me.'

'HOME?' echoed Sim, 'You canna do that. Why what would Elspeth say? She'd never let you keep him.'

He somehow made it sound as if the English boy were a wild creature Kirsty had found in the woods and she sensed Francis bristle.

Kirsty tried to assume her grand lady manner but it was a real effort. The adventure was over now and the only things she really wanted were her supper and bed

'Elspeth will do as I say,' she announced loftily, though in the depth of her mind she was rather doubtful. 'Come along.'

They made their way down the darkening valley with Kirsty walking between the two boys. A full orange moon was just appearing over the rim of the hills and the shadows were deepening into patches of indigo. Soon the bulk of the tower loomed before them, black and forbidding except for a few faint golden streaks from the narrow windows. Kirsty looked wistfully up at the topmost wishing she were already comfortably there.

'Shall I come in with you?' Sim enquired as they reached the main gateway.

Kirsty shook her head. 'I'll be all right now.'

'It's very quiet,' said Francis as Sim slipped away into the dusk, 'there doesn't seem to be anyone about.'

'Of course it's quiet. It always is when the men ...'

She was interrupted by the watchman on the gate who had heard their voices. 'Come awa ben Mistress Kirsty,' he ordered from the darkness, 'Make haste! I'm wanting to get barred up and off to my supper. That Sim's kept ye late again — and Elspeth's right vext. I'll be telling his uncle the morn.'

'Oh Eckie, please don't do that. I'm sorry. It was all my blame.'

'Why do you let him speak to you like that?' whispered Francis as they crossed the courtyard.

'It's nothing,' said Kirsty, 'he doesn't mean it. He's only cross because he hasn't been allowed to go on the raid with the others. He's getting old.'

'THE RAID? Are your people on a raid tonight?'

'Yes, But hush now. Here's Elspeth.'

Kirsty's nurse met them at the foot of the tower stairs and by the light of a torch burning in a bracket on the wall, Kirsty could see her usual kindly face looked like a thunder cloud.

'Mistress Kirsty! You bad wee besom! How often have I told you to be home by sunset! And who's this with you? It's never Sim?' She peered closely at Francis, 'Nay, it's a stranger lad. How did Eckie come to let him in?  Where did he come from?'

Kirsty tried to find words to explain but before she could speak Francis answered for her.

'She found me lost in the hills, good woman,' he said, 'and most kindly brought me back here.'

'What's he saying?  Who is he?' asked Elspeth in bewilderment, then very suspiciously, 'It sound like an English tongue to me.'

'He is English,' said Kirsty, 'and he was lost on the hills.'

'ENGLISH!' Elspeth gasped and crossed herself, 'The Blessed Virgin and all the Saints protect us!  Whatever possessed you to bring an Englisher here?  It's likely he'll be a spy.'

Oh dear, this was something about her new friend Kirsty had never thought of.

'OH no! No, I'm sure he isn't.  He **was** lost and I couldn't leave him out on the hills to die, could I?'

'No I suppose not.  But it would have to be tonight when the Laird's awa'.  Well bring him upstairs for a meal,' said Elspeth reluctantly,  'It must never be said we refused bite and sup to a stranger — even if he be English.'

'Still he seems a mannerly lad at least.'

she remarked more approvingly when they'd reached the top room where Kirsty's supper of bread and milk was waiting for her on the plain wooden table. For Francis, having enough sense to see that putting on airs wasn't getting him anywhere, had made Elspeth a low bow and then stationed himself behind Kirsty's stool and refused to take the other one Elspeth had drawn up for him, till the little girl was seated.

Elspeth then brought some more bread with a slice of cold meat and a beaker of watered ale, which she placed before Francis.

'I've had them put a truckle bed in the little room at the turn of the stairs,' she told him after they had eaten, 'it's where we store the peat for our fire — so that they don't have to bring it up every day. It'll no be like your fine rooms at hame no doubt, but you say you're going to be a soldier so you'll need to get used to roughing it — an' the worst we can do for you is better than the Lynn Pool.' she added grimly, for they had now told her the full story.

'Certainly it is,' said Francis, once more bowing gracefully to them both, 'I give you my thanks.'

'That one could charm a bird from the tree,' said Elspeth later, 'but I've turned the key in his door all the same. We dinna want him prowling about through night.'

She was washing Kirsty with the water which was always kept hot in a chaldron over the fire, and from the tone of her voice Kirsty knew she was still in disgrace. Whatever would her father say when he came back and found one of the enemy in his own house?

Kirsty didn't sleep well and towards morning a queer lowing and bellowing kept breaking into her troubled dreams. At last as the dawn light showed round the edges of the window shutters she woke up properly, but the noise continued and seemed to be all about the Tower. It puzzled her for a moment, and then she remembered. The raid must be over and the pasture round about full of English cattle.

As usual her first thought was for her father. Was he safe? Kirsty sat up and listened intently. After a few minutes she heard the men in the courtyard laughing and shouting to each other. All was well. It had been a successful night.

Then still worn out from the previous day's excitement, she rolled over and went to sleep again.

'Wake up, bairnie. Are you going to lie abed till noon?' Elspeth's voice finally roused her again. It was really morning this time for a long shaft of sunlight streamed across the room.

'Where...where's Francis?' Kirsty asked anxiously, feeling vext with herself. She had made such good resolutions last night to be up early and talk to her father before he met the English boy.

'He's with the Laird down in the hall — you've to join them later.'

'I'll go at once.' Kirsty tried to hurry her dressing.

'You must have your porridge first.' and though Kirsty protested she didn't want any, wasn't hungry, Elspeth insisted. So she struggled to eat, wondering all the while what would be happening to Francis. Her father was rarely angry with **her**, but he had a temper and would be tired after being out all night...

When she entered the great hall which was the main room of the Tower, she saw the remains of a meal hadn't yet been cleared from the table and Big Wat, with a tankard of ale before him, was sitting sprawled in his huge wooden armchair. He obviously hadn't been indoors long, for his pointed helmet was lying carelessly on the table and his great spear, almost twice the size of a man, was resting against the wall instead of being in the spear-rack as usual. Francis, looking very subdued, was seated on a stool opposite him.

Kirsty coming slowly forward and not quite knowing what to say, made a stiff deliberate curtsy. It was a formality she often forgot in her haste to get to her father and to see her do it now, made Big Wat frown.

'Come away, my lass. Elspeth's given me a sad tale of your doings — but you're not feared to face **me** are you?'

'Oh NO!'

Kirsty's barriers were down. She ran to her father and throwing her arms round his neck, gave him a hug and a kiss as she always did when he'd been away for any length of time. Big Wat lifted her to his knee and held her tight.

'I'm just talking to our — er, visitor here, about disobedience,' he said, 'and how it doesna only harm oneself but many other folk forby.'

'Oh Father, you do understand don't you? You know I simply had to bring him home,' pleaded Kirsty, 'You've always said the Tower should give shelter to strangers. He can't help being English — but you don't think he's a spy! Please say you don't — Elspeth does.'

Big Wat smiled. 'No, I think he's a foolish, headstrong boy who has caused a deal
of trouble — and may yet cause more — for
what to do with him I canna quite decide.'

'You'll not give him back to Nebless Nick,
will you?' begged Kirsty, appalled by the
very idea.

'I'd break our Border code of hospitality if
I did,' said Big Wat thoughtfully and studying Francis as he spoke, 'yet if I ask his
English friends to ransom him as is the
proper custom, Nebless Nick might hear of it
and say I was doing him out of the money,
So — the only thing seems to be to keep
Master Francis here a while — till spring
maybe — an' when he's forgotten about
we'll find a chance to slip him back across
the Border with nobody being the wiser.
Our folk'll not mention him if I forbid it.'

'Oh! But my uncle — my mother —
they'll be worrying about me.' Francis
protested.

'Weel, you should have thought of that
sooner.' Big Wat reminded him sternly,
'would you rather Nebless Nick had you?
It's only due to my lassie's playfellow that
you're here the now.'

'Oh Father,' Kirsty remembered Sim for
the first time since yesterday, and felt
suddenly ashamed, 'are you going to whip

Sim? Don't do it very hard.'

'He deserves it! Getting you into danger among the horses like that! I gave him a reet guid talking to — but a boy that can outwit Nebless Nick'll be a grand man some day. I told him to bide away from the Tower for a while and not be seen with you lest any of Nebless Nick's chappies ride this way. And now young Francis, are you willing to stop with us or would you rather chance your luck outside?'

'Indeed I wouldn't.' Francis gave a rueful smile, and made one of his grand sweeping bows towards Kirsty, 'I'll be content to regard myself as my lady's prisoner — and yours also, sir.' with another bow to Big Wat.

The reiver watched him gravely. Like Elspeth he was inclined to think elaborate manners were a sign of insincerity.

'Weel that's settled, and noo awa' with ye, bairns. It was a long night's trip and I'm gey tired.' Big Wat gave a mighty yawn and waved the children out of the room.

Kirsty took Francis's hand and led the way upstairs again, with a light heart. Things had gone even better than she had dared to hope and what she must do now was to make Francis feel happy and at home. She decided to begin by showing him her treasures.

Apart from a table and several stools, their large bare room was only furnished by a stiff wooden chair for Elspeth and a smaller one, which she'd almost outgrown, for Kirsty. There were also two chests. The larger held Elspeth's garments and various things they needed, but the little one was Kirsty's own and she lifted the lid with pride.

She took out her few possessions which were lying beside her clothes, and showed them to Francis one by one. There was a carved workbox with a little silver thimble and a pair of scissors inside. It was the most important thing for it had belonged to Kirsty's mother.

Then there was a doll which Big Wat had once brought back from Edinburgh. It too, was of wood, the body being all in one piece, but the arms moved and it wore a blue silk dress. Lastly, but by no means least, was the hobby horse Andrew had carved for her when she was small. It was merely a crudely shaped horse's head mounted on a stick, with a strip of cow-hide for its mane and large staring eyes marked in with tar. Kirsty had once adored it and still resisted Elspeth's attempts to make her give it to one of the village children. She imagined it might hurt Woody's feelings if she did so.

'But of course, I don't play with him any more now I've got a real pony.' she said.

'Oh, you've got a pony? What's it like?' Francis asked with interest. He hadn't said much about the other things.

'She's a dear little thing,' replied Kirsty, 'I love her so much! She's dark brown and her name's Lintie.'

'Lintie?'

'Yes, it's a bird you know. She was so frisky when she first came Andrew said she was blithe as a lintie — so we called her that.'

'Oh, that's it. You mean a linnet,' said Francis, 'she does sound nice. Can't we go and see her?'

'Of course, but let's go on the battlements first. I like looking down at all the cattle, and you'll see our view.'

From a small landing outside their room a continuance of the main road stairway led to the roof of the Tower. Kirsty ran gaily up it with Francis following her. Elspeth made no objection for there was always a watchman on the battlements whom she could trust to see her charge didn't get into any danger.

'There look!' cried Kirsty excitedly as she leaned over the parapet and pointed at a seething mass of cattle just beyond the outer wall. Their hides were shining in the morning sunshine like a heaving, tossing sea of brown, black and white.

'It's — amazing. Whatever do you do with so many?' asked Francis in wonderment.

'Oh, they go,' said Kirsty vaguely, 'off into the hills or to other people. They'll nearly all be away in a few days.'

'There's some sheep over there too,' Francis was still studying the scene, 'do your people take sheep as well as cattle?'

A merry laugh made the children turn round. The watchman who'd left his little shelter and strolled along to join them, overheard the question. 'We lift anything that isn't too hot or too heavy, young master,' he said proudly.

Kirsty greeted the good-looking trooper with delight — he was one of her favourites — but Francis rather pointedly turned back to the view and didn't answer. Though presently he spotted another curiosity which prompted a further question.

'What's that strange tree on the hillock over there — with the straight branches?'

'That's the hanging tree — for stringing up our prisoners,' said the young watchman with a grin, 'such as the spies Mistress Kirsty brings hame.'

40

He was only teasing as Kirsty knew but Francis flushed as he'd done the day before when Sim taunted him, and she hurried to intervene.

'Don't be silly, Dick!' she cried, 'You know Father never hangs anyone.'

'Ay weel, he's making a mistake this time.'

Kirsty caught the English boy's arm and drew him towards the door.

'Oh Dick, you are horrid! We won't stay with you any more. Come on, Francis, let's go and see Lintie now.'

Why **did** everyone have to be so nasty to Francis she wondered as they descended the Tower stairs. He was such a nice boy. She hoped he would stay with them for a long, long time.

## THE BEACONS BLAZE

Usually Kirsty disliked the onset of winter when the days grew short and mist came creeping through the valley to blot out the dear familiar hills. Everybody was so busy then, and all the conversation was about raids, and how many beasts should be killed and salted down in readiness for the lean months ahead.

But now she had Francis with her and what a difference his presence made. It was the happiest autumn she had ever known. Unlike Sim who was always having to go off and do some job or other, Francis was there all the time — at her beck and call from first thing in the morning till he bowed and kissed her hand as they said good-night.

She was pleased too that the people round about her seemed to have accepted Francis. At least there had been no further unpleasantness, though Elspeth still spoke sharply to him now and then, and old Eckie who had been unmercifully teased by the other men for having failed to notice he was letting in an Englisher, always scowled at Francis when they passed each other.

A long spell of bad weather had set in soon after Francis came to the Tower, but Kirsty was quite content to stay indoors with this fascinating new playfellow who had many good ideas for fresh amusements, and if Francis was ever tired of her insistent demands he managed not to show it.

She specially loved hearing about his family and sometimes wished she had **all** of them with her — most of the new games seemed to need more than two players and Elspeth wasn't much help.

'Nay, I'm too old for such capers,' she declared as Kirsty tried to persuade her to take part in Hot Cockles, a game which meant kneeling blindfold on the floor with hands open behind you and guessing who had slapped them. 'You want other bairns for these sports. What about having Sim in again? — the Laird won't mind now — and he's looking about for you. I saw him in the courtyard this forenoon.'

For a moment Kirsty was tempted to agree. It would be lovely to have Sim playing with her again. He and Francis would surely not quarrel now. Yes, he must come back. But before she could speak, Francis said: 'Another day, Kirsty. We'll have him in another day.' — and a glance at his face showed plainly that another day would be a long way off.

Elspeth must have soon realized it too. For after making several more attempts to re-introduce Sim into their company and finding every one blocked by some plausible excuse from Francis, she stopped mentioning Sim altogether.  Sometimes Kirsty thought rather guiltily that she was neglecting her old playmate, but was too afraid of stirring up fresh strife to protest.  Perhaps, she hoped, the boys would meet by accident some time and become friends.

Then one day she had a great surprise. She and Francis were alone upstairs and with Francis's encouragement she was enjoying a game of make-belief, when the door opened and in came Sim.

He was beaming all over his honest freckled face and after a moment's amazement Kirsty smiled back.  She had temporarily forgotten Francis's antagonism to him.

'SIM?'

'Good morrow, Kirsty!' he cried in response to her shriek of welcome, 'I asked the Laird if I could see you an' he said, aye, gang right up.  Eeh, it's been a weary time — an' I've such a lot to tell you... Our dog's had puppies, an' .... Why Kirsty —' he'd noticed her strange attire and the rigid way she was sitting on Elspeth's big chair, 'what are you wearing a cloak in the house for? — and isn't that one of Elspeth's caps? What **are** you playing at?'

'I'm on a barge!' she laughed, settling herself back.

'A barge? What's that?' asked Sim.

'It's a kind of boat,' explained Kirsty, 'It sails on rivers. The Queen of England always goes on one.'

'The Queen of ... Holy Saints! Kirsty, you're never playing at being the Queen of ENGLAND!'

His horrified face and voice made Kirsty realize what she was doing.

'It — it doesn't matter... It's only a game,' she faltered, but Francis broke in.

'And why shouldn't she play at being the Queen of England? She's a noble princess — and my King is a splendid knight who could beat yours any day — and they rule over a fine, civilized country where people are courteous and intelligent, not like this beggarly land where ...'

He got no further, for Sim, his face livid with anger, suddenly sprang back at him.

'Ye blackguard English loon!' he yelled flailing at Francis with his clenched fists. 'I'll teach ye to miscall us.'

Kirsty shrank down in her chair. This

wasn't the knightly conflict of her day-dreams nor the good humoured wrestling the men-at-arms sometimes indulged in. It was a REAL fight. With two furious boys attacking each other like young animals.

Round and round they went. Francis the taller and more agile, dodged about neatly — the fencing lessons he'd told her of, had made him very nimble footed — but Sim charged repeatedly, like a small fierce bullock.

'STOP! OH STOP!' cried Kirsty as they hurtled about the room overturning stools and Elspeth's spinning wheel, but they took no notice.

Then Francis struck Sim a blow which sent him reeling towards the fireplace. He knocked the iron cauldron hanging on its swey and the water splashed on to the fire, filling the room with smoke and flying ash.

This was terrible! In another minute somebody **would** be seriously hurt! Kirsty knew she must make them stop — there was nobody else to do it. And at that moment she caught sight of the broom resting against the chimney-piece.

Without hesitation she seized it and plunged into the frey. Screaming wildly she poked at the boys but they dodged around her as well as each other and continued their furious assault. Francis's nose was bleeding and Sim had a cut lip.

Kirsty was in despair for she found the broom too heavy for her to deal either of the combatants a telling blow, and she was now getting sadly buffeted herself. Then suddenly the broom was taken out of her hands and she heard Elspeth saying: 'Guid sakes, bairns! What goes on? 'Tis like the wars of Wallace and Bruce! Give over at once, I tell you.'

As she spoke Elspeth dealt Francis a blow which sent him sprawling to the floor and before Sim could attack again she was between them and chasing Sim out of the door.

As he stumbled towards the stairs the Scots boy turned round and managed to get the last word.

'Ye'll rue this, Kirsty! I'll no come nigh ye again! Yon southern windbag's makin a reet April gowk o' ye.'

Kirsty paid no attention. She was furious with Sim. He had spoilt her game and started the fight, and she was busy fussing over Francis whom Elspeth had lugged to his feet and thrust roughly into the big chair.

'Get out the dried herbs, Mistress Kirsty,' her nurse ordered calmly, 'You'll need to bathe his face with an infusion of woundwort

48

and comfrey. Then Master Francis must go to his room and stop there till we get this place decent again.'

Francis seemed very grateful for her ministrations. His face was horribly swollen, but he managed to murmur, 'You're a sweet little maid, Kirsty. A Scottish jewel. Katherine couldn't have tended me better.'

Kirsty's heart filled with pride and emotion, though she was sure that never again would she play at being Queen of England.

She was still very cross with Sim. She had never thought he could behave so badly. Hitting a prisoner — and being rude!

'I shall tell Father,' she said later as they were tidying the room. 'He ought to be punished.'

'I'd no bother if I were you,' replied Elspeth dryly, 'I had a wee keek out in the courtyard last time I was down and some of our fellows were standing round Sim laughing and patting his back. The Laird was with them and it looked to me very like he was laughing too! An' i' faith, bairn, I dinna blame them. It fair made my gorge rise to see you so taken with English ways.'

Kirsty sighed. It was plain that in spite of her previous hopes there were still plenty of

ple in the Tower who looked on Francis
th disfavour.

The weather changed for the better just as
Francis's black eye returned to normal, and
one bright crisp morning Elspeth said:
'What about a good ride the day, bairnie?
Yon pony o' yours is growing fat from lack of
exercise. Andrew's naught to do the now so
I've asked him to take you.'

During summer when the villagers were
tilling their little plots and there were plenty
of people about Kirsty ran freely in and out
of the Tower, but in winter when the paths
might be slippery from the frost or the bogs
swollen with rain, she went riding like a
proper young lady as Elspeth said, escorted
by grizzled old Andrew and such of the other
men as happened to be unoccupied.

'Oh good!' cried Kirsty. It would be
lovely to be out on Lintie again. Recently
she had only been able to take the pony for a
few turns round the courtyard when the rain
had held off sufficiently to allow her and
Francis to be out of doors for a while.
Otherwise she thought one of the stable lads
must have exercised Lintie. How glad the
pony would be to have a real long ride.
Perhaps they might even go the whole
length of the valley. 'But Francis must come
too. Of course he must.' It wouldn't be any

fun without him, but guessing Elspeth was about to say no, Kirsty added hastily, 'I'll ask Andrew.' and whisked down the winding stairs as fast as her legs could carry her.

She met Andrew at the stable door. 'Tak' yon Englisher, Mistress Kirsty! Nay, I dinna ken aboot that. The Laird's awa' the day so I canna ask leave. What if the lad gets off on us?'

'Oh, he wouldn't do that. I'm sure he wouldn't. Do let him come.' pleaded Kirsty, 'I won't enjoy the ride if he doesn't.'

'Nay, I'd never trust that one — but a' ladies must have a lapdog an' we ken weel the lad's yours. I'll be keeping him on the rein though, for safety's sake.'

Kirsty didn't quite like hearing Francis described as a lapdog but having got her way she ran back and told him he was being allowed to go.

'Hob the Lady's coming too.' she went on. Francis looked surprised. 'Who's he - she? I thought Elspeth and the serving maids were the only women here.'

'Why, he's one of the men — a new one!' Kirsty laughed. 'I thought I told you all our men have nicknames. Andrew is Black Andrew because he was so dark when he was young. Then there's one called Blanketlugs,' she giggled again, 'he once forgot there was to be a raid and stayed in bed. And of course, there's Dick the Deil,' she hesitated, 'the — the one who was on the battlements the first day you were here. He got his name for being a good fighter and he's really nice too. I wish he were going with us — but I may like Hob better when I get to know him.'

Francis wasn't at all pleased when he found he had to be on a leading rein. 'It's either that or ye stop at hame,' Andrew told him firmly, and Kirsty determined to compensate him for this indignity by making the ride as pleasant as possible.

If only it had been spring when the delicate white sorrel spangled the woods like pale stars, and the wild hyacinths which she called cratties, made patches of blue on the mossy forest floor; or summer when there was an ever changing play of light and shade among the leaves of the great trees and beyond the woods merry little rills sparkling on the heather-purple hillsides.

Now alas, as they rode slowly down the valley and looked at the view where Biglynn Burn joined the river, the woods were bare and brown, and the heather had faded. It was rather depressing but Kirsty enthusiastically pointed out all the interesting places as they trotted past them.

The ferny glade where Elspeth's mother had seen fairies when **she** was a little girl. The cairn where two knights were said to have fought each other to the death, and the old stone circle which the country people believed to be haunted.

Francis listened to all this with the same bored air he had assumed on the first day when she showed him her toys. Could it be possible, Kirsty wondered, that in England flowers bloomed all the year round.

'I suppose England must be much more beautiful than this?' she asked at length, rather wistfully.

'Well, it's different.' Francis brought his wandering attention back to her.

'But how is it different? Do tell me?' she persisted.

'Och! Mistress Kirsty! What a lassie you are for questions. Maybe some day there'll be peace atween oor twa countries and you can gang and see for yourself — but it'll no be just yet, I doubt.' Andrew sighed.

'Oh, that would be WONDERFUL! I could come and stay with you, Francis. Would you like me to?'

'Why, yes. — Yes of course.' Francis wasn't really listening. They were approaching the village beside the Tower and word had gone round that the English

53

prisoner was out for a ride, so there were quite a few people standing about to see them. Kirsty noticed a group of boys — Sim's friends most likely — making rude gestures towards them. But of Sim himself there was no sign. She hoped he wasn't going to cause any more trouble and looked rather apprehensively at Francis.

However he didn't appear to have seen the boys for he was staring hard at the little cobble-stone huts roofed with sods of turf, and suddenly he asked contemptuously, 'Why don't they build better houses?'

'Noo where would be the use of that when the English might burn them ony neet.' said Andrew.

'Dear me, you're not fighting **all** the time, are you? What do you do for amusement — or don't you have any?'

'Oh yes. We do,' said Kirsty glad to find him in a more conversational mood, 'at Yule we have a feast in the hall. It's such fun! Everybody comes — and there's a fiddler and they dance reels. And at Hallowe'en we roast nuts and tell fortunes.'

'But at other times?' enquired Francis and turned to Hob the Lady as he spoke.

'Weel,' replied Hob who was a quiet, thin young man with a pale rather cunning face, 'there's the football — and whiles we tak' a

54

turn at the cards or the dice in the guard-room. Come doon an' join us some neet if ye care, young master.'

'Ye'll have no time for gaming the noo,' said Andrew snubbingly,' it's coming on for the pride o' the moon — an' there'll be men's work to do at neets.'

Hob looked suitably crushed. Francis didn't say anything more and they finished their ride in silence.

As the winter closed in on them there was nothing Kirsty liked better than sitting by the hearth and making Francis tell her every detail about his own home.

Though he called it the smallest manor house in the county it sounded to Kirsty more like a fairy palace. Outside there was a garden with roses and fruit trees, and a terraced walk where a shimmering blue peacock strutted up and down, shrieking when it was going to rain. Inside the house the walls were wood panelled, the beds had curtains round them, and the windows were filled with a mysterious stuff called glass which kept out draughts but let daylight in.

Kirsty couldn't understand how such a thing could be, but it was plain that coming from a comfortable home like that, Francis found their chilly northern winter hard to bear. Though Elspeth had made him a pair of deerskin leggings and they had found him a warm cloak which he wore most of the time. He'd been in summer clothes when he arrived and they'd been almost torn to pieces by the rough handling he'd endured.

Now as he sat crouched towards the fire on the other side the hearth like a shivery old man, Kirsty looked pityingly at him.

'Couldn't we have the window shutters closed now?' she asked, knowing well that Francis was too proud to mention it himself.

Elspeth glanced up from her spinning. 'Yes, if Master Francis will shut them, I'll go for the milk for your supper.'

She often gave Francis this task because he was a few inches taller than her.

As Elspeth left the room Francis carried a stool to the window and sprang up. Before he drew the heavy shutter into position he paused and peered through the narrow opening.

'Holy Saints, it's cold tonight! And what a lot of stars there are... so low down too. How queer! Oh, that's not a star — it's a light on the hill!' He stretched further till he could look round about. 'Why Kirsty, there's lights on **all** the hills. What is it?'

'Oh, get down, Francis, and let me see!'

The children changed places and as Kirsty struggled to see without clambering into the window space as she sometimes did, the watchman on the roof above them gave a shout. It startled Kirsty and she jumped back to the floor.

'Whatever's happening?' Francis exclaimed.

'IT'S A RAID!' she cried, 'The English are coming! Didn't you hear the watchman say: a bale! a bale! Those lights are the beacons.'

'Of course they are. Why didn't I think of that? Oh, I must have another look!'

Francis climbed up to the window again and craned his head out as far as he could. 'There are two fires on the big hill now.'

'That means they're getting near.' Kirsty was beginning to be a little scared, 'Oh, do come down Francis and close the shutter.'

'No, I want to see...' he was beginning, when Elspeth came back into the room.

'What's going on? Come awa' fra the window, Master Francis. Your supper is ready.'

'But Elspeth, there's a raid! The English are going to attack us... the beacons are lit. Oh Elspeth, what's going to happen? They've never raided us before.'

'Save us, bairn! We've had these visitors every winter. But knowing how you were about raids I've always got you to bed in good time and a wee drop of soothing syrup in your milk made sure you wouldn't wake till all was over. Only tonight yon silver tongue beguiled us.' Elspeth frowned at Francis which Kirsty thought was rather unfair. She had enjoyed hearing him talk about his home as much as either of them. 'Come along now and get your suppers.'

'Oh, I can't. I can't eat anything,' said Kirsty, 'I — I'm frightened. What shall we do if the English come?'

'Now how could they touch us with these six foot thick walls and all our stout lads to defend us? You're being foolish, bairn.'

'They — they might scumfish us.' Kirsty was fast working herself into a panic.

Francis who had been unusually silent, now put his arms round her. 'What do you mean Kirsty! Scumfish us? What's that? You mustn't be frightened. I won't let them touch you.'

Kirsty clung to him. 'It — it means they might put straw in the passage — burning straw, Francis — and — and smoke us out!' Her eyes were wide with fear, 'I heard the men talking about sieges one day — and that was what they said.'

'Nonsense, Mistress Kirsty!' Elspeth was growing impatient. 'How often have I told you not to hang about listening to the men.

Surely you don't think the Laird would let our enemies get so close? Your father's daughter should have more spunk!' she took hold of Kirsty firmly and led her towards the table. 'Sit down to your supper at once. I must go and see if those lazy wenches downstairs have water boiling and food prepared. The village folk may come to take refuge with us any moment. And Master Francis, keep that shutter closed — we don't want a stray arrow in here. Now behave yourselves, bairns, everything'll be all right.'

She bustled away. Kirsty looked at the meal she had no appetite for, and then at Francis. To her amazement he had lost his hopeless old man expression and was smiling happily.

'Oh, Kirsty! Kirsty! Isn't is SPLENDID! I've been dreaming of this. They must have come to rescue me.'

Kirsty forgot her fears in astonishment at the way he had changed. 'No, I don't think so. They'll be looking for cattle — they'll be wanting some back.' she replied practically.

'Then this is my chance! I must go back with them! I MUST get away, Kirsty!'

It was as if Kirsty's world were falling about her ears. She knew Francis would have to leave her some time, but... but not yet... and certainly not in this way... not with those nameless strangers out in the dark who were threatening everything she cared about.

She had vaguely imagined that some day far, far in the future, they would all ride in state to the frontier and Francis would bid her a sorrowful farewell, vowing that though they lived in opposing countries he would still remain her true knight and faithful friend.

'You — you can't go. Not — not like this. You — can't leave me tonight.'

'But I've **got** to, Kirsty. Don't you see it's my chance at last? You must be brave and help me. The ladies in old romances always helped their knights — and just think how worried my family must be. Your father always said I could go.'

That was true. Kirsty was quiet for a moment. She couldn't bear to loose him... but was she perhaps, being selfish? He had a mother and sisters who might be crying for him every night.

'You — you won't forget me? she asked slowly.

'Oh no, Kirsty dear heart. Of course not. I'll always love you. I'll love you next best to Clarissa. But you **must** help me.'

'What — what have I to do?'

'Come with me and don't say anything. I've got an idea.'

Holding her hand he cautiously led her downstairs and into the great hall. There was nobody there except Griselda, Big Wat's peregrine falcon, sitting glaring at them from her perch in the corner.

'Look,' said Francis keeping his voice low as if he didn't wish even the bird to hear him, 'you see your father's hunting horn, I'm going to take it down. I've learnt the hunting calls and if I blow the notes for Come-to-me, the English'll know I'm here. Then when they find out who I am they'll do everything I say. Don't be frightened, Kirsty, I won't let them hurt any of you — and I'll tell them how very, very good you've been.'

Signing to her to be quiet, he went to the wall and with some difficulty lifted down the big horn. As he did so, Kirsty thought she heard something like a grunt or a groan — but it must have been a noise from outside.

'Now, come on.' Holding the horn Francis began to make his way back upstairs. Kirsty rather reluctantly followed. She was beginning to see flaws in his plan. From all she had heard about the English it didn't seem likely they would behave as Francis expected — but he must know best.

He was older than her — and they **were** his own people.

They came out on to the battlements with only the star-studded sky above them and their own beacon burning brightly in its iron basket. Kirsty was startled to hear Francis swear softly as he quickly lifted the horn to his lips. He had forgotten there would be a watchman in the little shelter by the beacon.

At the same moment a harsh voice said; 'Get out of the way, Mistress Kirsty! and she was pushed roughly against the parapet, as a man who had crept up the stairs behind them, hurled himself at Francis and tore the horn from his hands.

'GOT YE! I ken't we couldna trust an Englisher!'

It was cross old Eckie. His shout and the little scream Kirsty gave, brought the watchman running from his shelter.

'Come to relieve me, Eckie? Good man! Eh, what's going on? D'ye want some help?'

'Nay, I'm managing. Get off quick … ye'll miss the fun. Ay, an' tell Gib the turnspit tae fetch some irons.'

In spite of his age Eckie was very strong and Francis was no match for him. Kirsty watched in horror as he twisted the boy's arm behind him and roughly dragged

Francis to his sleeping apartment.

'Oh, don't hurt him, Eckie!' wailed Kirsty, 'Please don't. You're being cruel!'

But Eckie didn't care. He was getting his own back and hurling Francis down on his bed, held him there till a few minutes later an ugly, gangling youth came in swinging a set of rattling chains.

Kirsty shrank back into a corner, weeping softly. She hated Gib, an uncouth, dim-witted creature whose main job was turning the heavy iron bars on which huge joints of meat were roasted before the fire. He was always black with soot and covered with the grease which had splattered on him while he worked.

It was awful to see him bending over Francis and helping Eckie force Francis's hands and feet into position and clasp them with the fetters.

She desperately wanted to stay and comfort the captive, but Eckie just pulled her away, and even gave her a little smack as he pushed her towards her own quarters.

'Ye'll leave him be noo,' he growled, 'I'd tak' a strap to ye, ye wicked wench, if ye were my bairn. Siding wi' the English against your ain folk!'

The room was empty so she knew Elspeth must be still busy. Kirsty felt very much

63

alone and wondered what was happening in other parts of her home. Had the villagers come in for refuge? And was Sim among them? Whatever would he say — and Elspeth — when they heard she had tried to help Francis escape? The story would be going all round now unless the English were actually attacking. Her other worries had almost made her forget about the raid, but now she thought she would just take a peep out and see what was happening.

Opening the shutter she saw many people were moving about in the courtyard but the beacon fires had died down. They were safe. Their strong walls had protected them once more, just as Elspeth said. But what of the trouble within? Suddenly Kirsty felt she couldn't stand anything more that night — especially her nurse's scolding. She undressed quickly, drew the bedcover over her head and sobbed herself to sleep.

In the morning there was only one porridge bowl on the table. Kirsty looked anxiously in the direction of Francis's room.

'He's had his food,' said Elspeth who seemed tired and harassed, 'the Laird's going to deal with him later.'

'Can't I just speak to him?' asked Kirsty.

'No.' Elspeth was firm, 'Nobody's to talk to him till your father's seen him.'

Oh dear, poor Francis! What was going to happen to him now?

Kirsty couldn't settle to anything, She fidgeted about, taking her toys out of the chest and putting them back again, till she hit on the idea of getting her needlework and sitting on a stool near the door, where she pretended to be very industrious while listening for any sound from Francis's room.

It was a long time before she heard two men come upstairs, then there was a creak as they opened the door and finally the jangling of chains as Francis was led away.

Dropping her sewing Kirsty darted after them — she didn't want Elspeth to stop her — but once out of the room she slowed down and reached the great hall well behind the others.

Warily she peeped inside, not wanting to reveal her presence till she saw what was happening. The scene reminded her of the first morning Francis was there. Only this time Big Wat was **really** angry, not just half pretending to be, and instead of sitting at ease he was standing fully armed and raging at Francis in a manner Kirsty had never seen before. The English boy stood cowed and broken spirited before him, but — in spite of her agitation Kirsty noted this crumb of comfort — at least Francis wasn't wearing those awful chains now.

'You ungrateful young fool!' the reiver stormed, 'D'you think our wild Border prickers would care aboot your southern notions of chivalry? Why, even if it had been a Warden raid led by Lord Dacre himself, I doubt if he could have protected you once his followers broke in here.' Big Wat's voice cut like a knife, 'Have **you** ever seen men with the blood-lust in them? Mad to kill? Hungry as wolves for plunder? I could die sword in hand as my fathers did before me — but had you thought what would have happened to Kirsty — to Elspeth — and the other helpless folk who find refuge in our pele?'

Kirsty still shamelessly eavesdropping and now trembling herself, could see Francis droop like a wilting harebell under the torrent of furious words.

'There's but one thing that counts on these Border marches — and that's the strong blade with a steady arm and cool brain behind it — and ruthlessness — the will to slay when necessary ... Come with me, lad.'

Big Wat turned abruptly, left the hall and descended the Tower stairs. Francis followed, with Kirsty well out of sight behind them. Surely her father wasn't going to kill Francis — it had sounded very like it.

She tried to prepare herself to dart forward and plead for her friend but instead of going outside as she expected, her father paused in the vaulted room on the ground floor of the Tower which was always kept empty so that the villagers and some of their most precious livestock could crowd in if needs be. Big Wat crossed this apartment and opened a narrow door in a corner. It led to a dark little chamber Kirsty had always believed to be a store-room. It was piled with boxes and barrels but there was a clear space at one end. Big Wat went straight to this, and stooping, lifted an iron grating over a round hole in the floor.

He indicated that Francis should look down it, and Kirsty slinking round the boxes and barrels, looked too. As she did so one of Elspeth's expressions flashed into her mind — black dark — that's exactly what the hole was! She heard Francis give a gasp of fear and he shrank back.

'You — you — wouldn't put me in there?' he stammered.

'I WOULD.' said Big Wat still at his sternest, 'I'd do worse than that to protect my bairn and my home.'

Kirsty gave a sob. She couldn't help it.

'So you're here, are you? And you acted like a babe last night I'm hearing. I'm ashamed to ken o' it! Get back to your nurse! Back to Elspeth at once!'

Sorrowfully Kirsty turned away. There could be no pleading, no appeal now. Her father was the Laird and must be obeyed, and as she went towards the stairs she could still hear Big Wat going on at Francis.

'Just remember lad, this dungeon's called an oubliette which I'm told is a French word for forgotten. If you were down there and anything happened to me — if I were dead or wounded say, — our folk would find it very easy to forget you ...'

As she dragged herself reluctantly away Kirsty hoped desperately that Francis would be reasonable and stay quietly with them. She could see now that his attempt to escape had not only been foolish but doomed to failure from the start. It must never happen again.

She resolved that when things returned to normal — if they ever did — she would beg Francis to wait patiently till her father released him. He must never risk being put in that dreadful oubliette!

And now there was Elspeth to face.

When Kirsty at length reached their room, trembling and somewhat sick, she found

Elspeth exceedingly kind, petting and comforting her charge while she assured her that Big Wat's anger wouldn't last long.

Francis came back to them very subdued, and sulked for several days while Kirsty tried hard to coax him into a good mood. Then she asked him not to try to escape again and he replied: 'I won't!' and looked at his wrists where the tender skin had been chafed by the fetters, 'besides —' he added sadly, 'I'm not likely to get a chance now.'

Other people too must have thought he'd learnt his lesson, for soon after this their rides out were reassumed as if nothing had happened.   And one beautiful morning Kirsty's happiness was complete when Andrew actually let Francis off the leading rein, though he warned him sternly that any tricks would result in an arrow in his back. But Francis behaved perfectly and the children enjoyed a glorious race along the level haugh beside the river, with Hob the Lady, who was again accompanying them, galloping along side.

They were a merry party, laughing and wind-blown, as they returned to the Tower. Then when they entered the courtyard Andrew rode ahead to speak to someone who was calling him, and Francis who had suddenly gone quite quiet for the last five minutes, exclaimed in tones of the utmost sadness, 'Back to prison.'

'Och, dinna say that, young master,' replied Hob taking the rein of Francis's mount, 'we dinna think the worse o' ye for trying to escape — an' look here, if ye ever weary o' petticoat rule, just come doon to the guardroom, as I telt ye afore. We'd be weel pleased tae see ye.'

Francis gave Hob a strange long hard stare. 'Thanks,' he said shortly, 'I might do that sometime.'

A few nights later while Kirsty was having her bath, Francis did go to the guardroom and stayed till after she had gone to bed.

He must have enjoyed it very much for gradually he began going down almost every night. Kirsty who didn't like being left out of anything was puzzled and annoyed.

'Whatever do you do?' she asked one day.

'Oh, we've grand fun,' Francis answered carelessly, 'we play for the gold coins in my purse and somebody different wins them every time.'

'How exciting. I'd like that. I wish I could play too.'

'Well, you can't.' Elspeth joined in firmly, 'Whoever heard of a young lady of gentle birth playing at the cards with her father's jackmen.'

It didn't seem at all fair, and Francis **was her** prisoner. He should play with her all the time. But when he began disappearing in the daytime she was really cross.

'That boy needs to be with other men.' Elspeth had tried to explain.

She was thinking of this now as she sat by the fire one frosty evening in early spring. What a strange winter it had been. Her wish to keep Francis with her had been granted but she often felt she'd lost him after all. For besides spending as much time as he could in the guardroom, he had become quite friendly with the men, and Kirsty would see him standing out in the damp to watch them play football, or going with Hob the Lady to an archery practice. Indeed he seemed so settled she half imagined he would stay with them for ever, and perhaps be her father's page or something...

It was queer too, that since the terrible night when Francis tried to escape she seemed to have lost her fear of raids. Perhaps it was because she was growing up at last, for the beacon fires had been lighted on several more occasions during the dark months, though maybe with Biglynn Tower being out of the way, the English had not made a direct attack on it again.

There was a raid taking place somewhere this very evening. For only a short time ago the watchman had called; 'A double bale! To horse! To horse!' meaning that somebody had sighted the English and lit two fires as a warning. Then their own men had ridden in force to help repel the invaders, and Francis, crying out, 'I won't be long, Kirsty!' had raced off to see them start.

'He can't keep away from Hob!' Kirsty said to Elspeth who was sitting at the other side of the fire, spinning as usual.

'Jealous again?' smiled Elspeth and then went on, 'I dinna ken what's possessed the southerners to come as late as this. If the men dinna rest the night they'll no be fit to start ploughing the morn — an you'll no get your ride out, my lady.'

'Oh, don't say that!'

Andrew had promised her a very special ride, their last one before everybody was busy with the spring cultivation, and Kirsty was looking forward to it so much.

They were going far into the hills to visit an elderly couple who kept a herd of exceptionally fine goats. Elspeth warned her it was too early in the year to expect kids but Kirsty hoped there might just be one. She was sure she could coax her father into buying it.

The last time she'd gone Sim had been with her, Kirsty was trying to forget that, for she rarely saw Sim nowadays. He had kept out of her way since his fight with Francis.

Oh, why didn't Francis hurry back? The flat piece of wood on which he'd been trying to mark out a Nine Men's Morris game before he ran off, was still lying on the floor. She picked it up idly. She didn't know how to play — and if Francis didn't come soon there wouldn't be time to learn before she went to bed.

Elspeth was already putting her work aside. 'Come now and get undressed. The lights are just about out.'

'No, not yet,' begged Kirsty, 'not before Francis comes back.'

'Huh, he's not hurrying. Maybe he's off to his bed.'

'He wouldn't — not without saying goodnight. I expect he's in the guardroom.'

'Not likely when they're all awa' but if it'll pacify you I'll go and see.'

Kirsty heard her tap at Francis's door, then open and close it rather sharply before she descended the stairs.

'There's only Eckie sitting his lone in the guardroom and he hasna seen the lad.' Elspeth reported when she returned. 'I told him to send him up if he did.'

'Perhaps he's hiding then,' suggested Kirsty for certainly Francis wouldn't stay anywhere near Eckie, 'I know where he'll be!'

They had played hide and seek a few days previously and Francis had found some dark corners she hadn't noticed before. So she ran through the various rooms and peeped into every one.

At last she came to the ground-floor and glanced out at the courtyard. Everything was coated with a fine sprinkling of hoar frost and there were glittering pools of golden light from the lanterns carried by a few people who were still working about. It was bitterly cold and she was just going to go back inside, when she heard shouting at the main gate. It opened and a man rode hurriedly in.

'Andrew? Wha's Andrew?' he called as he jumped from his horse, brushed past Kirsty and dashed upstairs. She wasn't interested. The men were always rushing around, and another idea about Francis had occurred to her. He might just be on the battlements. She had forgotten to look there.

She didn't see the man or even think of him, as she rushed back and opened the door to the top of the tower.

'Is Francis there?' she called.

A gush of biting air and a sharp answer were all she got.

'No, he isna, Mistress Kirsty — an' he'd be daft if he was! Get that door shut or Elspeth'll have something to say.'

Dejectedly Kirsty turned away. There was no sign of Elspeth so she slowly began to go downstairs once more. But she had barely reached the next landing when she saw Elspeth and Andrew standing close in conversation at a turn of the stairs. They both looked so terribly serious Kirsty's heart gave a leap of fear. What could have happened now?

'Mistress Kirsty! There you are!' Elspeth came up and Andrew, muttering, 'Ay weel, — I'll see ye later.' took himself off.

'Now then, bed,' said Elspeth in business-like tones. 'You've been wandering about long enough.'

'No — no —not yet!' cried Kirsty, 'Not till Francis comes. What's the matter? Has something happened to him?'

'Nay, he's all right, but you must away to your bed now and no arguing.'

Perhaps she had better, Kirsty thought as she sipped the hot milk Elspeth insisted on. If Francis was all right they would meet in the morning — and she must be up early to go and see the goats.

She fell asleep almost at once, her last thoughts being a confused jumble of Francis — having an accident? — old Tib and Jock — and dear little kids skipping about on the braeside.

When she opened her eyes again sunlight was shining through the sides of the window shutters. It was going to be a bright day, a lovely day — the day she and Francis were to see the goats. Then she remembered … there had been something queer going on last night … or had she been dreaming? Had something happened to Francis — and Elspeth given her a sleeping draught to keep her quiet? Then there had been a raid, hadn't there? She didn't think there had been any fighting but perhaps Francis had been hurt — or slipped on the stairs — he was always complaining how steep they were — and broken his leg. She must get up at once and see. If he was hurt he would need her.

She dressed quickly and threw a cloak round her for the morning was chill. Elspeth wasn't about so she went across the landing to the door of Francis's room.

'Are you awake, Francis?' she asked tapping softly.

There was no reply. She tapped again but

there was only the hollow sound of an empty room, so she gently opened the door. The bed was unoccupied — at least that meant he wasn't ill or hurt.

She made her way to the great hall. Everything was still quiet and there was nobody about except a few servants bringing peat and logs for the fire. When they noticed Kirsty they gave her a queer look and then turned quickly away as if pretending they hadn't seen her.

Kirsty was frightened — something **had** happened — and she couldn't bring herself to run after them and ask what it was.

Then she thought — Hob! Hob the Lady. Of course. They were so thick, he and Francis. Of course Francis would be with Hob. She would go outside and ask some of the men where they were.

Just as she got downstairs another thought struck her. The oubliette! Suppose Francis had done something wrong again — tried to escape perhaps. Had her father put him in the dungeon — and was that why everybody was behaving so strangely? Oh, he couldn't have — her father would never be so cruel. But he'd meant what he said, she knew that.

Oh, if Francis were really down that horrible dark hole she would beg and beg for him to be let out. In her mind she pictured herself going on her knees to Big Wat and weeping like a lady in one of Elspeth's stories till her father gave way.

She entered the gloomy little room with her heart beating quickly.

'Francis,' she called again, 'Francis, are you there?'

Nothing answered and going near the hole she saw a big wooden barrel was standing over it. Could she move it? Kirsty pushed with all her might and luckily it seemed to be empty and not as heavy as she feared. Making a great effort she managed to push it to one side and peered down into the hole.

'Francis!' she said for the last time. There was nobody there! She felt a great surge of relief. How silly she had been! Wasn't Elspeth always telling her not to let her imagination run away with her? Of course her first idea must be right — Francis would be with Hob.

'Where's Hob the Lady?' she demanded imperiously of the first man she met outside.

He looked slightly bewildered and bleary-eyed as if he'd been up all night. 'Why I — I dinna ken, Mistress Kirsty,' he replied awkwardly.

'Oh, never mind.'

A fresh thought had struck her. Hob had

an old aunt or grandmother he sometimes stayed with on the other side of the village. She would get Lintie and ride there — that would be quickest — and she could ask everyone she met on the way.

Elspeth would be angry no doubt, but never mind that. Francis didn't seem to be in the Tower and she **must** find him.

She ran to the little shed where Lintie was stabled away from the rest of the horses. She would saddle up and be off before anyone could stop her.

Kirsty pushed open the door — and got the surprise of her life! LINTIE WASN'T THERE!

She stared at the empty shed. Could the pony have been moved elsewhere? No, Lintie's saddle and bridle had gone too. Kirsty had a dreadful sense of foreboding. Somebody must have stolen Lintie!

Almost crying she turned and raced across the courtyard and straight into the arms of Elspeth who had come to look for her.

'Elspeth! Oh Elspeth! Lintie — Lintie's gone — and — and Francis.'

Kirsty was fairly sobbing now.

'There, there, bairnie. I ken — I ken... Come away inside quick. The Laird's up in the room waiting to speak to you.'

'Up in the room?'

Kirsty stared at her through tear-misted eyes. This was something else unusual. Her father seldom came upstairs — she always went down to him.

She found Big Wat sitting on the largest of the two chests because Elspeth's chair wouldn't fit him. He appeared tired and the scar on his face stood out more vividly than ever. But he held out his arms and lifted Kirsty to his knee.

'Oh Father, Lintie's lost — and I — I think she's s-stolen and — and Francis h-has d-disappeared.'

'Ay, ay, my doo (dove),' said Big Wat, 'can you be brave noo? Borderers are always brave, aren't they, and Elliots most of all?'

'Um,' Kirsty nestled to him.

'I ken Lintie's been stolen — an' I ken wha took her too,' his arms tightened round Kirsty, 'It was Francis!'

'FRANCIS? OH NO!'

'The bale fires called us out last night, do you remember? And did you no see a man come back later?'

'Y-yes.' Kirsty nodded, events of the previous evening beginning to form a pattern in her mind.

'Weel, he came to tell Andrew that two

riders wha'd left hame with us at the back o' the troop, had broken off an' gone their way across the hill. We sent a couple of arrows after them — but they'd had too good a start. One o' them seemed to be on a pony.'

'Francis?'

'Ay, Francis — and Hob. They must have had it planned a fair while. He took Lintie because he ken't she wouldna be missed soon. The raid was a false alarm, bairnie. When we got to Corbiesbrow, the rallying spot, we learnt the English had never stirred. Ye ken Hob came fra the Debatable Land (a neutral zone at the head of the Solway Firth) where a' the outlaws live. Some o' his friends there must have fired the beacons. But dinna fret for Francis, sweetheart, he was like the swallows which men say go off to follow the sun to the south. He just didna fit in wi' us. Let's just hope Nebless Nick never gets to ken o't or there'll be trouble.'

'Oh Father, he needn't have taken Lintie like that. I'd given him her if he'd asked.' Kirsty's head went down on to the padded leather jacket, Big Wat, like most reivers, often wore instead of body armour, and she wept bitterly.

'There, my darling, my wee doo. Dinna greet so. I'll find ye another pony.'

'I — I don't want one,' sobbed Kirsty, 'it wouldn't be the same. Oh Father, it's what Francis did that hurts. He promised not to leave me.'

'Ay, I ken bairnie.' Big Wat's hand crept to his dagger out of force of habit. He could have killed Francis for grieving Kirsty. 'I ken fine. There's naught worse than treachery. A friend breaking a faith pains worse than a sword cut — and pray heaven, you'll never feel that.'

'A draught of poison in a golden cup,' agreed Elspeth who was watching them with an anxious face. 'Come cheer up, bairnie. Summer'll soon be here — an' then you'll forget him.'

But Kirsty didn't. Francis's callousness had given her too much of a shock, and at first she had little chance to forget.

Everybody was talking about it. How shameful of Hob the Lady to help a prisoner escape and what kind of bribe had Francis offered him to do it? They all agreed it must have been a large one.

Kirsty felt she wanted to close her ears and hide. Why did they have to go on so?

Elspeth made various suggestions in the hope of raising her spirits. They could still visit old Tib and Jock — there would certainly be kids now. Andrew could take Kirsty up in front of him, and she, Elspeth, ride pillion with another man. But Kirsty had lost all interest in this.

Well, they could have Sim in, what about that? Kirsty exclaimed in horror at the mere idea. She remembered his bitter last words to her. They had come true. Francis had indeed made a fool of her. She could never face Sim again.

The weary days dragged on with Kirsty growing more pale and listless all the time. 'I'm feared the bairn's going into a decline,' she heard Elspeth say to someone.

Then one morning that lively young man, Dick the Deil, came bounding upstairs, put his head round the door and shouted: 'Hey Elspeth! Andrew says to tell ye there's a showman in the village wi' a monkey an' a dancing dog. They're a' resting the noo, and the fellow's breaking his fast, but the wee beasties'll perform at noon.'

Kirsty who was sitting by the fire putting a few languid stitches into the hated needlework, lifted her head and listened. This was something exciting at last.

'I mislike such gentry,' said Elspeth, 'but he's just what we're wanting. Tell Andrew I thank him kindly — you too, lad. We'll be there.'

'Ay, I knew ye'd be glad to ken.' Dick the

Deil ran off, whistling cheerily as he went.

Kirsty jumped up. Her troubles for the moment actually forgotten. There were plenty of wandering pedlars and travelling showmen in other parts of the country but they seldom risked coming to the Borders in case they got caught up in any of the fighting. So this man would be something very special, a treat to be talked about for months afterwards.

And a monkey! She had never seen a monkey, but Francis had told her one of his cousins had one as a pet. No, she wasn't going to think of Francis. She wouldn't let him make her miserable any more. She was going to enjoy the showman and his animals.

Elspeth tried to comb her hair but Kirsty fidgeted excitedly. It was so thrilling!

'Patience, bairn,' said her nurse, 'you're going to see the performance not be one of the showman's troop. Here, 'she went on, 'You'll have to give him something, so I'll lend you these,' she went to her chest and took a couple of copper coins out of a small leather bag, 'the Laird'll pay me back the night when he returns fra the hunting.'

Though she spoke sharply she smiled as she put the money in Kirsty's hand. It was the first time Kirsty had looked like her old self since Francis disappeared.

When they reached the village they found all the people clustered in an open space in front of one of the larger cottages, and with pleasant greetings they stood aside for Kirsty and Elspeth to get to the front. Immediately Kirsty looked about for the monkey.

Oh, there it was! A comical little thing with chestnut brown fur, a small cunning face and tiny hands which clutched the bars of its wicker-work cage.

And there was its master, a little wiry man with a shrewd face and twinkling eyes rather like the monkey's. He wore a ragged red and yellow suit and was sitting on the ground drinking a tankard of ale, while he told the villagers jokes. A white terrier with black spots lay between his legs.

But apparently he knew who Kirsty was, for as soon as she got into her place, he sprang to his feet.

'Ah, blessed day!' he cried, 'The noble lady of the castle comes to grace our show! Quick Jacko, make your reverence to our patroness!' He flicked open the monkey's cage, and with laughter and exclamations from the crowd, it darted out. The man had a tiny green hat with a feather in the band which he clapped on the animal's head, and snapping his fingers in the direction of Kirsty, said: 'your best bow, Jacko, please!'

It stepped towards her, swept off the hat with a minute paw and made her a low courtly bow. The villagers cheered and Kirsty was delighted.

'Now you, Mistress Spot!' said the showman, and the dog sat up and begged, covering its eyes as if praying as it did so.

Then the man made the animals run round and round him, with the monkey riding on the dog's back and occasionally jumping through a hoop bound with coloured ribbons, which he'd produced from his bundle.

After that the animals rested while their master asked the terrier questions and Mistress Spot replied by barking once for 'yes' and twice for 'no'.

'Wha does she ken't reet answers?' asked one of the villagers in amazement, but the showman only laughed and bringing out a small flute began playing such a merry tune Mistress Spot rose on her hind legs and the animals danced a jig together.

When they stopped, the man laid down his flute and looked hopefully round the crowd.

'Give him your money,' whispered Elspeth, 'or we won't see any more.'

Shyly Kirsty held out the coins and the man signed to Jacko to collect them in his doll-sized hat. Jacko bowed politely and returned to his master. A few of the villagers also gave a coin, but most promised to give the showman some oat-cakes or a piece of cheese when he was ready to depart.

The man next began performing himself, turning cart-wheels and somersaults, and walking on his hands. Jacko copied every-thing he did and Mistress Spot sat watching with a disdainful air as if she thought they were being too silly for words.

At last the showman was so tired he sat down again and played another tune which made the animals run round once more, jumping over each other in turn as if they were having a game of leapfrog. They moved so quickly it was fascinating to watch them. Kirsty laughed and cheered with the rest of the children. Then at the height of the fun, somebody on the outside of the crowd suddenly shouted; 'ENGLISH!'

Everybody turned. 'It's the hot trod,' cried another, 'they'll no bother us.'

Down where the valley widened out a party of riders led by a baying hound, were crossing the moor-land. They carried smoking lumps of peat on the points of their spears as a sign they came in peace.

'I dinna trust them,' said one of the older folk, 'We'd best get oot o' sight!'

Though generally raids took place in the winter there was always a certain amount of stealing across the Border, and anyone who lost cattle in this way, was allowed by law to pursue them into the other country. Only those concerned were supposed to be in the chase, but sometimes people who came along for the excitement caused trouble.

This happened now. As the riders swept on their way several men left the main band and turning aside galloped furiously towards the village. They had noticed the crowd round the showman.

'They're comin'! Flee! Flee! FLEE FOR YOUR LIVES!'

The villagers scattered like frightened sheep. The showman, who had popped Jacko back into his cage at the first word of alarm, swiftly gathered the rest of his belongings and disappeared among the cottages. But the villagers knowing the enemy would burn their homes as soon as look at them, ran towards the safety of the Tower.

Kirsty ran with the rest, but the weeks of staying in and fretting, had taken their toll. Her legs felt as if they were made of wood.

Elspeth caught her hand, and muttering broken prayers, panted along beside her.

The English were now pursuing the villagers with hunting calls. It was VERY FRIGHTENING! All round them the other women and children were crying and screaming.

Presently the crowd in front of Kirsty seemed to move apart and far ahead she saw Sim with his family. Without thinking about it she called his name.

'SIM!'

He couldn't possibly have heard her through the tumult but something made him glance back. Immediately he pushed the two small children he was leading, forward, and turning, raced back to Kirsty. His rough, strong hand grasped her free one and she had both him and Elspeth helping her along.

As the foremost people reached the Tower a group of men led by Dick the Deil, came out and running to either side of the fugitives, shepherded them towards the entrance. The English seeing they were about to loose their prey, let fly a hail of arrows. The Scots fired back, and everybody screamed louder as the arrows hissed through the air.

But the villagers were quickly getting into

safety now, only a few yards separated Kirsty from her home. They were almost there. She drew a breath of relief which turned into a cry of pain as something hit her leg. She stumbled, let go of Sim's hand and looked down. Her skirt was pinned to her leg by an arrow!

'HELP!' cried Elspeth, 'The bairn's wounded.'

Kirsty leaned against her, too terrified to move. Then one of the men, she was not sure which, picked her up. Somebody else broke off the long shaft of the arrow to prevent it catching in anything, and she was carried crying through the crowd. At the gate she was handed to Andrew and found herself being taken up the safe, dark, familiar turns of the staircase till Andrew laid her gently down on her own bed with a pillow supporting her injured leg.

She heard Elspeth call for hot water, and then as her nurse cut the skirt away from the wound, Kirsty fainted.

How long she was ill she never knew. For days she tossed and turned in fever, calling hopelessly for Francis and babbling incessantly about Lintie, raids, and blazing beacons and even sometimes recalling her terrifying childhood experience when she saw Robbie's dead body brought back to the

Tower.

Occasionally she was dimly aware of people bending over her. Andrew, Dick, and others of the men, Elspeth and some of the village women who were skilled in nursing the sick, Sim with his freckled face wrinkled with anxiety, and most of all, her father.

At last came the day when the fever left her — and it was as if a dark cloud had lifted from the Tower. The men went about chaffing each other, the servants laughed and sang at their work.

But after only a few more days there was silence again. A deadly silence this time, for Elspeth had told them that Kirsty's wounded leg wouldn't support her and it looked as if she might never be able to walk again!

## THE WOUNDED BIRD

Sim wandered along the moorland track, moodily kicking any loose stones that lay in his way. He had come up here alone on the hill to think. For he was worried, dreadfully worried about Kirsty.

For months now she had lain in bed, pale, listless and unable to walk, and nothing he, or Elspeth, or the men-at-arms (who had all tried to think of something) or even the Laird himself, could do, would rouse her.

Why, just at Eastertide when a sudden cold snap made Elspeth send the maids scampering for fresh eggs and basins of new-fallen snow, so that she could make snow pancakes, Kirsty hadn't shown any interest — and Kirsty used to love snow pancakes! Sim clenched his fists and muttered an oath he'd heard the men use.

It was all the blame of that cursed Englisher... If only he'd never come to the Tower, charming Kirsty's love fra her ain folk and making a quarrel between them. Many times since then he'd almost wished he'd stuck his knife into Francis instead of the horses or let Nebless Nick throw the boy into the Lynn Pool — but that would have upset Kirsty — and when it came to the point, Kirsty's wishes were all that mattered to Sim.

Her illness was such a mystery. Elspeth, who'd tended many sick people, said they were sometimes powerless for a long while after a severe injury. But what comfort was that? It just seemed to Sim as if his merry little playmate who'd run about and climbed with him, had died and left a white, hollow-eyed changling in her place.

Maybe that's what it was! Perhaps the Englisher had cursed them before he left or perhaps some other evil influence had bewitched Kirsty. Sim considered the matter. If that were so it would need something special, a mighty strong spell, to make her better. A wise woman could probably do it — but who would tell him how to find such a person? They were so chancy to deal with and would he actually have the courage to approach one?

At that moment Sim suddenly noticed he wasn't alone on the hillside. A tall figure in a black cloak and white robe was walking through the heather some distance below him. Sim stared hard at this unusual stranger. Yes, he was right. It was a priest!

Sim spat. He'd only once before seen a priest, and that was soon after his family had moved to the village, when a grim sour-faced man had come preaching to the people, telling them to repent of their sins and cease fighting and killing. It had made some of the women and children weep but the men were quite unmoved. They had seen so much death and cruelty that the hell fire the priest talked about couldn't frighten them.

That priest hadn't stayed in the village long and from jokes Sim overheard, he thought someone had killed him.

Sim felt rather uncomfortable. What if this priest were seeking revenge? Perhaps Kirsty's illness was part of a curse which would fall on everyone. On the other hand priests were supposed to be gey sib (friendly) with the saints and to know holy words, so was it possible, just faintly possible, that he might be able to help Kirsty? Was it too fine an opportunity to miss? Sim knew he daren't overlook any chance but he still hesitated. Would the priest mind being stopped by a mere boy? What about the hell fire if he were displeased?

Sim plucked up his courage — he would have to risk all that. He was a Borderer, son of a Borderer, and must never show fear in the face of an enemy.

But as he ran after the stranger Sim thought he'd rather fight somebody human even if they were English or as ugly as Nebless Nick, than encounter spirits whether good or evil.

Sim's heart was beating unpleasantly fast as he drew near the man and heard him singing to himself in words the boy couldn't understand.

'Sir priest!' called Sim when he was within hailing distance, 'Sir priest, I pray ye, let me speak wi' ye?' better be polite to begin with he thought, but putting a hand on his knife. 'Ken ye aught aboot healing folks?'

The man turned round to meet Sim and the boy saw he had a kindly, lined, weather-beaten face.

'I do have some skill in that way, but it is slight I fear,' he said, 'who is it that's ill?... or stay... how do I know this isn't a trick? That you're trying to lure me into a trap or ambush? — Not that I've anything worth stealing, my lad.'

'Oh, I'm no! On my honour as a Scot!' cried Sim indignantly, 'Here, tak' my knife as token o' guid faith.' He held out the weapon hilt formost. 'Ye see it's my master's daughter — The Laird o' the Tower yonder's bairn. She's just a bit lass, but she was shot in the leg by the black-hearted English last time they attacked us.'

'How long ago's that?' asked the priest, 'are you telling me the wound won't heal?'

'Nay, it's healed but she still canna walk,' explained Sim, 'I thought ye might have a charm to cure her.'

The man looked as if he were trying not to laugh.

'You young heathen! I don't work magic. Well, I'll come and see the child, though by what you say, I doubt if I can do much.'

'Tell me your master's name?' he enquired presently as they walked along together. 'And yours?'

Sim told him. 'And what do they call you?' he asked boldly.

'I'm known as Brother John, a humble monk of the Cistercian Order, and I'm on my way to the Abbey of the Blessed Virgin Mary at Melrose. Do you know where that is?'

'To the east, is it no?' said Sim not in the least interested. They were nearing the Tower and he was wondering what sort of welcome they would get.

It didn't look promising. 'Weel, young Sim, what pyet's (magpie's) this ye're bringin' us?' the first man they met asked with a curious stare.

'No another spy?' suggested somebody else.

Brother John threw back the hood of his cloak to reveal his shaven head and held out a rosary to the men. 'I am a man of peace and no spy,' he said, 'Bless you my sons.'

Sim didn't wait to hear more, he had spotted Andrew in the distance and rushed to tell him what he'd done.

'Ye're reet, lad. We canna miss a chance.' he said much to Sim's relief, 'The Laird's awa' the noo but I'll tak' responsibility for letting the guid priest ben.'

Then going up to Brother John, he greeted him warmly. 'Welcome, reverend sir. We'll be reet grateful gin ye heal oor wee mistress. Wi' ye're permission I'll just step up the stair ahead o' ye an' warn Dame Elspeth, the nurse, what's afoot. The lad kens the way.'

As they slowly followed him across the courtyard, Sim suddenly caught the monk's sleeve. Another worrying thought had struck him.

'Ye'll mind an' no frighten her,' he warned urgently, 'she greets gey easy the noo — an' ye'll no tell her o' hell fire, like the priest wha came afore ye? He made a' the women feart. I'll no stand that wi'

Kirsty! Gin ye do aught to harm her, I'll find another knife an' cut ye' to pieces. I will that — if it taks' me years — ay, an' gae to hell mesel' afterwards.' He ended ferociously.

Brother John merely patted his shoulder in a friendly way.

'Blood-thirsty warrior! Come, lead on. A boy that cares so much for his friend'll never go to hell. Don't worry.'

They found Kirsty lying in bed as she always was nowadays, with a hand-woven blanket over her.

When she saw Brother John she half raised herself — and screamed.

'A GHAIST! A GHAIST!'

She went on screaming in a way that made Sim feel like holding his ears and rushing downstairs. He'd never seen Kirsty like that before.

He made a grab at the monk, crying fiercely, 'Ye mind what I telt ye afore!'

'Peace! Peace!' Brother John put him gently aside, and did the same with Elspeth and Andrew who had rushed to Kirsty's bed. 'Peace, my child. I'm not a ghost. See...' he softly touched her hand, 'I'm flesh and blood like you are — and I've come to help you.' He sat down beside her. 'Now no more tears. What about letting us see a

100

smile on that pretty little face?'

Kirsty made a watery effort.

'There that's better. Now tell me, have you ever heard of the Blessed Virgin Mary, Mother of Our Lord Jesus Christ?'

'Y-yes,' faltered Kirsty, surprised, 'She-she lives in heaven — and my mother lives with her.'

'Well then,' said the monk, 'you see everything's all right. Those ladies sent me here. Isn't that wonderful! And what about letting me see that sore leg?'

He pushed the covering to one side and closely studied the white scar. Then, very gently he moved her legs.

'Don't! Oh, don't do that! You mustn't try to make me stand,' cried Kirsty in another panic. 'They did once before and I just fell down!'

'All right! All right! I won't touch them again.'

He replaced the blanket and glanced at the anxious watchers. 'I think it must be what my dear friend, Brother Infirmarian who tends the sick, would call a distemper of the nerves.' He turned back to Kirsty. 'Rest now, poor little wounded bird — and let's talk of something else. Do you hate the English as much as your fire-brand friend here does, my child?'

Kirsty stared at him. This was getting near the grain. She remembered Francis, but the weeks of lying still had taught her something.

'They're mostly bad,' she said thoughtfully, 'but not all. An English girl Father met on — on — one of the raids, sent me this.' She took out a tiny silver cross which was hanging round her neck, 'She was a very poor girl. Father told me all about it. She'd long yellow hair and big blue eyes, and her clothes were all ragged but she stood up and asked questions about me. Father said she was much braver than the boys who were with her.'

'MARGERY!' exclaimed the monk, 'Margery, David and Robin, by All the Saints!' He began to laugh. 'Ha! Ha! Wait till I get home and tell Robin what your Father said. That'll take him down a peg!'

'Who's Robin!' Sim burst in curiously, looking at Brother John in amazement. His fear of hell fire had almost vanished. A priest who laughed like that and spoke so kindly would surely not harm anyone.

'Another hot-headed little varlet like yourself, my son,' replied Brother John giving him a pat on the shoulder, 'I'm very fond of Robin — and David too. David is Robin's adopted brother and they are both apprenticed to Robin's father to learn woodwork. Margery is their friend — but I'll tell you about them tomorrow. Our invalid's had enough excitement for one day. May I come again, my child?'

'Oh yes, do — please,' said Kirsty who had begun to like this quiet-spoken stranger.

'Ye mean ye'll bide here?' asked Sim.

'Yes, for a day or two at least — my superiors won't mind when they know the reason — if somebody'll put me up for the night, that is.'

Ye're welcome to stop in oor bit cott, your reverence,' said Andrew quickly, 'my wife's no so active as she was but she'll do her best to mak' ye comfortable.'

'A bowl of porridge and a bit of floor to sleep on is all I need,' and with that Brother John kissed Kirsty's cheek and blessed her before following Andrew downstairs. Sim lingered a minute to say goodbye.

'I hope we dinna get preached to all evening,' he said with a grimace which made her smile.

Next morning Sim was back at the Tower before the gate opened. His later observation of the monk had increased his good opinion of Brother John — but that was not to say he had done anything for Kirsty.

To his delight she was sitting up and looking brighter. Sim experienced a great feeling of relief. Yes, the priest's spell must be starting to work! And sure enough Kirsty's first questions were about Brother John.

'What's he been doing? Did he preach to you?' she asked.

Sim chuckled. 'Losh, he hasna had time! He's been so busy. He mended Dame Beattie's milking stool; helped the men dose a sick cow; chopped wood for old Widow Nixon and carved my wee sister a doll fra a bit stick. The daftest thing —wi' a muckle heed an' squint eyes —an' she loves it! I'll get her to fetch it an' show ye.'

Kirsty listened eagerly. 'Perhaps he's a saint,' she suggested, 'Elspeth once said they go about helping people, didn't you, Elspeth?'

'Yes,' said her nurse and whispered to Sim, 'keep talking, lad.' while she went on aloud, 'Now you must be fresh when the good priest comes again, so we'll have a bite to eat first. I've had them kill a chicken and make some broth — and Sim'll share it wi' us, won't you?'

Sim was only too willing. Poultry were so precious they were rarely killed for food, and this would be a great treat.

The children chattered happily over the meal, and afterwards Elspeth tidied Kirsty and put on her best dress. They had hardly finished when Brother John arrived.

Then followed the most enjoyable time they had had since Kirsty was ill. As he'd promised the monk told them about his other little friends who lived in the English village under the walls of the monastery which was his home. How the young waif, David, risked his life to save a sheep from the quicksands, and how Margery had a pet goose called Esmeralda to whom she was devoted.

Brother John was an excellent story-teller, changing his voice for the different people and pausing at the most exciting parts so that the children begged him to continue.

'Oh, must you go?' they both exclaimed when at length he rose to depart.

'I'll be back tomorrow,' he assured them, 'and tell you a story from the Holy Scriptures.'

'Lovely! That'll be something to look forward to,' said Kirsty, 'I do like stories.'

Sim and Elspeth exchanged smiles. This was a great improvement. Kirsty was regaining her interest in life.

The monk continued visiting her for

several days and she grew to have much confidence in him.

One afternoon when Sim hadn't been able to join them she spoke of something that worried her.

'D - Do - do you think' she asked very hesitantly, 'that God let the English shoot me as a punishment for my sins?'

Brother John who was explaining the rites of the Church, stared at her in amazement, then his lips twitched. 'Why child, what terrible sins have you been committing to make you think that?'

'I was horrid to Sim.' Kirsty burst out, determined to get her confusion over quickly, 'I stopped playing with him — and quarrelled — badly. And he's been so good. Look how he brought you to me — even though he was frightened of you... and... and that — that other time when — when the English chased us — and the arrows were flying,' she covered her face with her hands, 'he came back to be with me. He's a real true friend, and — and Father and Elspeth both say Borderers **never** desert their friends... but Francis was so different — so exciting — and — and I thought he loved me.'

'Francis?' inquired the monk, 'who's Francis?'

106

Kirsty told him the whole story. Brother John's face grew stern when she reached the part where Francis took Lintie.

'And you've never heard anything more?' he asked as she finished.

'No. Father says Hob will be hiding with the outlaws in the Debatable Land.'

'H'm, the pony was chestnut you say? Well, I'll see what I can hear — but don't count on anything. I'm sure your father will get you another when you're better.'

'It's just — just if I could only know Lintie was all right. That — that nobody was being cruel to her — because I'll never be able to ride — or walk — again. They all say so.'

'They? Who?' Brother John spoke sharply.

'Why, the women who came to help when I had the fever at first — and Elspeth — I see her crying sometimes — and Father, he looks as if he'd like to cry too but he goes out of the room quickly.... and Andrew's the same... and Dick... and...'

'Come,' said Brother John bracingly, 'these good people may know a great deal about sickness — but there **is** Somebody even more powerful than your father — and you know Who, don't you?'

'God?' said Kirsty softly.

'Yes. When His Son, the Lord Jesus, was

on earth He healed people much worse than you. So we must pray that you may regain the use of your legs and that He'll give you peace of mind. Will you always remember that?'

Kirsty sighed. 'I'll try, but it'll be hard.'

Big Wat had been away all this time but one day when Brother John was in the middle of a thrilling story about the Children of Israel escaping from Egypt they heard the clatter of mailed feet and Kirsty's father strode in.

'They're telling me downstairs that we've a visitor.' he said, as Sim, Elspeth and the monk moved aside to let him come to Kirsty's bed.

'Oh, Father,' she cried after she'd kissed and hugged him, 'Do ask him to stay here. He's such a good, kind man!'

'Ye've done the bairn a deal o' good, reverend sir, We'd be maist honoured if ye'd lodge awhile within oor puir walls.'

'I thank you,' Brother John inclined his head politely, 'It cannot be. My superiors expect me at Melrose by the full moon and that's but three days off now.'

'They say ye've come fra Holm Cultram in Cumberland. 'Tis a fair Abbey,' said Big Wat slowly, ... I've been there ... if ye'll but heal my bairn, good priest, I'll see oor riders ne'er molest it again an' I swear to send a score o' fat beasts to Melrose forby,'

'It's not for me to heal the child,' answered Brother John, 'God must do it in His own time — and let's pray it may be soon. But I must depart tomorrow. I shall get a very severe penance if I stay longer.' He made a mock dejected expression at the children.

'Oh no! Please not yet.' Kirsty protested.

'Yes, I'll have to, I'm afraid. But you'll think about my stories and tell them over to Elspeth, won't you? She'd enjoy that, I expect.' He winked at Elspeth who immediately said there was nothing she'd like better.

Next morning Kirsty bade a tearful farewell to Brother John while Sim went with him as far as the end of the valley to carry the salt meat and bannocks Elspeth had packed for his journey. The monk also had three gold coins in his pouch which Big Wat had given him to put in the alms dish at Melrose Abbey.

At first Kirsty tried faithfully to remember all the stories and the prayers she had learnt, but gradually as her new friend's visit slipped into the past, she lost interest. The days became as long as ever and there didn't seem the slightest sign of her regaining her health.

She was nearly as listless as before and Sim was again becoming frantically worried, when one day, quite out of the blue, Brother John came back.

He went straight to Kirsty's room just as he used to, said good-day to Elspeth, blessed them both and sat down in his old place by Kirsty's side.

'Now, my child,' he said after he'd replied to her ecstatic greeting and inquired about Sim and everybody else,' you'll see how God answers prayers. When I got to Melrose I found my brethren there very puzzled by a letter they'd just received. It had come all the way from the south of England, passed on through the various religious houses of our Order till it reached Melrose — and can you guess who it was addressed to?'

Kirsty stared at him in wonder and slowly shook her head. She had heard about letters but never seen one before.

'Then listen. To Mistress Christine Nancibelle Elliot of Biglynn Tower in the Borders of Scotland.'

'ME!' gasped Kirsty.

'Yes, you. And just imagine how surprised everyone was when I said I knew the lady and had been visiting her in her own home. But now can I open and read it to you? But you mustn't be upset what ever it says for I think it's from Francis's family. These three circles on the seal are meant to be millstones I believe, and isn't that the crest of the Milverton's?'

'Yes,' said Kirsty, 'he told me about it.' She was trembling now, partly with excitement and partly with fear. Letters brought news and what was she about to hear?

'To Mistress Christine Nancibelle Elliot,' read the monk again and then came a long formal greeting which she hardly understood and didn't really listen to. She was trying to puzzle out how words got on to paper — and anyway it didn't seem to concern her after all.

Then Brother John's voice changed and she heard something that did matter — very much indeed.

*'Dear little maiden,'* he read in tones so low and tender, Kirsty had a mental picture of a sweet-faced lady bending over the letter, *'this is to beg you not to grieve for your pony, Lintie, which our son, Francis brought here in all safety. The little mare now dwells in a pleasant meadow beside this our house, and none rideth her except our youngest daughter, Clarissa, who is, I think, of an age with yourself, and much loves the animal, and feeds her with apples in due season.*

*My son would have written to you himself but his father has sent him abroad to learn the skill of arms, and thus asks you to excuse him and he will ever be your true knight always to command.*

*We shall ever remember you with affection and gratitude and would have sent you a trinket of some worth but feared it might be stolen on the way, whereas this sent by the good Fathers may reach you happily and be of more lasting value, which is the prayer of your servant, Mary, wife of Sir William Milverton, Knight of the Manor of Fayrehurst, in the County of Oxfordshire, who joins with all our family in wishing you well, and your continued good health and long life.'*

A confusion of thoughts chased each other through Kirsty's mind as Brother John finished the long letter. Lintie was safe — what a blessing! And she was quite pleased for Clarissa, who'd sounded a nice child, to have her if she couldn't. Besides in that lovely green meadow (Kirsty believed England had perpetual summer) there would be no danger from stray arrows and no rough work to crush Lintie's spirit. But was she as pleased to have news of Francis? To know he'd deceived his own parents as readily as he had her, making out Kirsty had

112

given him Lintie when he'd really stolen the pony in such a hurtful fashion?

A gentle hand touched her arm. 'Don't you want to see what she's sent you?' asked Brother John holding out a small packet.

'Oh yes, of course.' Kirsty came back to the present. She took the parcel and carefully opened it. Inside was a little brown, leather-covered book. She turned the leaves wonderingly. They were covered with black lettering but on every page the capital letters had fascinating small coloured pictures painted inside them.

'How pretty! What is it?' cried Kirsty.

'A portion of the Gospel according to St. Matthew,' explained the monk, 'the story of the life of Our Lord. You'll like that.'

'Oh, but you know I can't read,' said Kirsty disappointedly, 'nobody can here.'

'You can learn.' Brother John told her in his bracing fashion. 'We'll begin now. See, here's another gift. I got Brother Jerome, who is good at woodwork, to make it specially for you.'

He showed her a shallow box about the same size as the book. It was filled with wax and inside the lid was a piece of parchment covered with clear horn.

'These are the letters of the alphabet,' Brother John pointed to writing on the parchment, 'and you can copy them on to the wax tablet like this...' he produced a pointed thing which he said was a stylus, and showed her how to use it. 'There, I shall teach you something fresh every time I come and it'll be so interesting, won't it?'

Kirsty was quite surprised to find how quickly she learnt. Before Brother John went away again, she could write her own name and recognise many letters in her book.

At first it seemed strange books were written in Latin instead of everyday speech but the monk assured her she would soon get used to it. Kirsty believed him for her confidence in Brother John was increasing with every visit. So many things he'd told her had come true, though of the most important, being able to walk again, there was no sign whatever. Perhaps as Sim always said when she was down-hearted, this particular spell was one that took a long time to work.

Kirsty felt much happier now and was so taken up with her new occupations she didn't find the days nearly as tedious as before. Besides practising her reading and writing she discovered the wax tablet was also good for drawing on. So she made an endless series of comic faces which she and

Sim laughed over together. She even took a fancy for doing her needlework — but it was Sim who put the idea of a lute into her mind.

The children were poring over the Gospel book one day when they noticed a picture of an angel playing a musical instrument. Sim immediately wanted to know what he was doing. Kirsty wasn't sure either so they appealed to Elspeth who said the spirit must be making sweet music — that was a lute in his hand, she was sure of it.

Sim turned to Kirsty excitedly, 'Eeh, the varra thing! Ye must hae a lute, Kirsty! Ye could play it sitting there an' mak us a' merry. Why, folk would come far an' wide to hear ye. Get the Laird tae buy ye one, Kirsty. They say there was a message fra Edinbro' asking him tae gang soon.'

'Oh, do you think so?' Kirsty laughed happily. She would love to have a lute, she just knew she would — and perhaps, if Elspeth allowed it — she could have some of the village children — Sim's small sisters maybe — come in and dance to it. She was sure she could teach them just as the showman had done his little dog.

'Father! Is it true? Are you going to Edinburgh soon?' she cried, when Big Wat came to say his usual good-night to her.

'Um, news travels fast it seems,' he said

115

with a frown, 'Aye, I'm awa' the morn, bairn.'

'Oh, then …' Kirsty was too excited to notice he seemed displeased, and launched into her plans for a lute, '… and it must have red ribbons on,' she insisted, 'Elspeth once worked for a lady who had one, and she says it had red ribbons. You will get me one, won't you, Father?'

'Bless ye, my doo,' Big Wat smiled at her enthusiasm, 'I'll get ye a lute if I can.'

'I knew you would! Oh, I can't wait! Will you be away long, Father?'

'Maybe a fortnight — or less if all goes well.'

'Then hurry back,' she begged. It seemed a long time to wait but Edinburgh was a good way off. Kirsty was still thinking about the lute as she fell asleep.

'Aye say your prayers, sweetheart,' Big Wat said as he kissed her farewell next morning, 'an' mind o' me.'

'Of course. I always do.' Kirsty was rather surprised. He wasn't generally so serious. 'But you won't forget the lute, Father?'

'Nay, I'll no forget.' He gave her a final embrace and turned away. 'Tak guid care o' my bairn for me, Elspeth.'

'Dinna fret yoursel', Laird,' Elspeth

116

replied, 'I'll guard her with my life.'

Whatever was making them so solemn Kirsty wondered impatiently as she threw her father a last reminder about the lute. 'I want one with red ribbons on.'

'With red ribbons,' repeated Big Wat dutifully, and giving her a strange long look he quickly left the room.

Elspeth brought Kirsty a piece of stick and every night they cut a notch on it. But when the fourteenth day passed and Big Wat had not returned she began to be restless.

'He must have been delayed. Maybe his horse went lame or something.' Kirsty thought Elspeth sounded a bit anxious herself, 'He'll be here soon, bairn.'

The waiting was especially trying as Sim was not able to come in just then. Though strangely enough Big Wat hadn't taken more than a couple of men with him, Andrew was keeping the others busy with their seasonal tasks, and Sim had to help. How Kirsty wished she too could run about and see what was going on.

Soon her impatience turned to anxiety when one day she thought she heard Elspeth say to Andrew who had come up to see them, 'I must tell the bairn soon.'

Tell her? Tell her what? Kirsty was

almost beside herself with worry. Were they keeping something from her? Had something happened to Big Wat? Could he have fallen in with the English? No, that wasn't very likely, Edinburgh was a great city, the capital of Scotland, with fine houses and shops, and the king's own castle and palace. Her father would be safe there. She mustn't let herself get fanciful again. She had promised Brother John to try and control her imagination.

But still she couldn't throw off the feeling that something was wrong — and when she tried to question Elspeth her nurse only returned the most evasive answers. What ever could it be they were hiding from her?

It was a great relief when Brother John made one of his unexpected appearances. Now I'll get the truth at last thought Kirsty as the monk settled down to hear her lessons. The minute Elspeth goes out of the room I'll ask him if anything's the matter, if he scolds me for being silly I shan't mind.

They had barely opened the Gospel book to find the text she had learnt, when they heard many horses trotting into the courtyard and loud voices shouting commands.

'FATHER.' Kirsty gave a delighted yell, 'At last!'

'Nay, calm yourself, bairn. It's not the

Laird I doubt. There's more men there than he took with him.'

Disappointed Kirsty settled herself again. If it wasn't Big Wat she wasn't interested. There was always coming and going among men.

But her lessons hadn't got much further on when they were once more interrupted. This time by men's harsh voices on the landing. In a minute the door was pushed roughly open and there stood Nebless Nick!

He looked just like a great black-bearded giant as he paused with a shaft of afternoon sunlight from the narrow window falling full on his evil disfigured face.

'Oh no!' before she could stop herself Kirsty gave a little whimper of fear and stretched out her hand to clutch the monk's habit. Elspeth who had been moving restlessly about the room since they first heard the horsemen, came over to the bed-side.

Brother John removed Kirsty's grip and rose to his feet.

'Sir,' he said in the gentle authoritive manner he could assume at will, 'I do not know you, but this child is sick and must not be distressed, Pray retire and conduct your business with some other member of the household.'

He stepped towards the intruder as he spoke.

'I'll retire ye, ye auld black corbie (crow)!' said Nebless Nick, 'Tak that!' and he dealt Brother John a blow which knocked the monk senseless to the floor.

'He's fettled!' said Nebless Nick triumphantly, and motioning the men who were with him to stand by the door, he advanced to Kirsty's bedside. She shrank back against her pillows like a terrified little rabbit. A quick glance at her nurse had shown her Elspeth's face ashen white. Brother John still lay in a huddled heap. Kirsty wondered if he were dead.

'So ho, m'lady! Ye're no as spry as ye were last time we met. Noo harken, I'm takin' command here an' I want tae ken wha was that lad wi' ye wha pricked the horses yon day? I'll hae him whipped till the blood rins — or ...' Nebless Nick paused and moistened his lips, 'maybe hanged'd be better. Yon dule (sorrow) tree o' yours hasna borne fruit for a lang while.'

Kirsty shuddered. She felt as if she were having a nightmare.

'No — no — you can't. F-father won't let you.' she managed to say. Oh, if only Big Wat were there.

'He's no likely tae stop me,' Nebless Nick

replied, 'he'll be biding in Edinbro' for a bit, my lass, if the King's Grace's Privy Council hae ony sense in their silly noddles — sae I'm master here — an' ye'll do as I bid.'

'He's not — he will — you're not ... You're just trying to frighten me,' stammered Kirsty and looked imploringly at Elspeth.

Her nurse didn't fail her. 'Leave the bairn alane,' she said bravely, 'The Laird's aye angered if she gets upset.'

'Haud ye're tongue, woman!' Nebless Nick turned on her in a fury. 'I'm tellin' ye Big Wat's in the dungeon o' Edinbro' Castle — an' stopping there!'

Kirsty couldn't believe her ears. Her father — a prisoner? In that great grey fortress she'd so often heard about, high on its impregnable rock above Scotland's capital — oh no!

'...treason ... the King's ain orders ...' Nebless Nick was still raving on, ' ... he's slighted me gey often ... I'll see he pays noo. Come on lass, tell me who yon lad was? I meant tae have him some road. Speak up quick - an' I'll leave ye be.'

He reached out a dirty, hairy hand to grasp Kirsty's shoulder and her nerves snapped.

'I WON'T! I WON'T TELL YOU! YOU CAN'T MAKE ME!' she screamed, hurling herself towards the side of the bed where Elspeth stood. Her nurse caught her in a tight embrace, and settled her back with a reassuring hug and a meaningful look which seemed to say, don't worry I'll get him a message first.

But Nebless Nick had noticed and his fury knew no bounds.

'NAY, YE'LL NOT WARN HIM! I'll see tae that!' he stared round the room, 'Lock the door? Ay, an' ye'd gang tae the window. An' I canna spare a guard tae ye. Here, fetch a rape!' he bellowed at his followers and a few minutes later one of them appeared with a coil of rope.

'Tie the woman tae the bed yonder,' their master ordered, pointing to the open door of the small apartment where Kirsty slept before her illness and which Elspeth now occupied instead.

Kirsty cried as the men seized Elspeth, dragged her across the room and flung her on the bed. Nebless Nick stuffed a kerchief into her mouth and they tied her so firmly she could neither move or speak.

Then he turned back to Kirsty with a spiteful leer. 'That's reet. The priest's silenced — best tie him wi' his girdle tae mak' sure — an' ye canna move. But wait till we catch the lad. I'll hae ye carried doon tae see what happens!'

With that he stumped out of the room, aiming a kick at Brother John as he went The men followed, slamming the door behind them.

Kirsty huddled among her wrappings and wept hopelessly. She knew without doubt that Nebless Nick would carry out his threats. He had borne them a grudge too long. If he caught Sim he would hang him for sure.

Oh, why was there nobody to help? She raised her head and heard Eslpeth moaning as she vainly tried to free herself from her bonds. The only other sound was the far off noise of riders passing in and out of the courtyard. Kirsty wondered if their own men were safe and what they were doing. If only she could get in touch with one of them.

Time was going on. Nebless Nick's foll-owers would be hunting for Sim. Never before, in all the months of her illness had Kirsty felt so helpless.

'Oh, I MUST do something!' she thought desperately, 'I MUST SAVE SIM!'

On a sudden impulse she shoved back the blanket and sprang to the ground. For two wild, wobbly steps her legs supported her, then she flopped like the broken-winged bird Brother John had once called her. But

'I CAN WALK! I CAN!' she thought excitedly as she dragged herself across the room. Dear Brother John, he always said I could. She tried not to look at the silent figure of the monk as she crawled towards Elspeth.

She reached up to the bed, but alas, the men had done their work thoroughly. The knots were too tight for her small fingers. If she just had a knife. Looking round she spotted her workbox standing on the small chest. There would be scissors in it! She crawled back to the chest, pulled herself up and got them. They weren't very big and Kirsty patiently sawing through the rope, dreaded every minute that Nebless Nick might return.

At last the final strand snapped, Elspeth's hands were free and she tore the gag from her mouth.

'Keep quiet, bairn.' she whispered as they struggled to loose the rope from her legs.

'Elspeth! I can walk!' Kirsty said softly. Too excited to be silent longer.

'Can ye, bairn?' Elspeth was so flustered she couldn't appreciate the good news, 'Well, wheesht while I see what's happening.'

She went to Brother John, turned back his robes and felt heart and pulse.

'He's living, praise be!' she announced. Then lifting Kirsty placed her on the floor beside him.

'Bathe his face, bairn. I'll no be gone a wee minute.' She thrust a cloth and a mug of water taken from the crock which always stood handy on the landing, into Kirsty's hands and left the room.

Timidly Kirsty dabbed at Brother John's poor bruised forehead and presently she was rewarded by seeing his eyelids flutter, and a few minutes later he opened his eyes properly, murmured something which sounded like, bless you, and closed them again.

Kirsty continued her work, but in an agony of suspense. It seemed **hours** till Elspeth returned, though when she did, she was looking more cheerful and like herself.

'How is he?' she asked and Kirsty told her.

'Good,' Elspeth smiled at last, 'I had luck too. I ran right into young Mysie — she's a canny lass that, got a head on her shoulders.'

'Yes?' Kirsty nodded. She too liked sensible red-haired Mysie, one of the younger maids.

'She'll pass on word to warn Sim — I can trust her — but she says Nebless Nick's men are everywhere. We canna get out by the

126

main door — an' his lordship's sitting in the Laird's ain chair supping our best wine.' She paused and gave Kirsty a thoughtful look. 'They've forgotten the tower stair. D'ye ken who's on guard up there?'

'Dick, I think,' Kirsty whispered back, wondering what was in Elspeth's mind, 'I heard him whistling **Blue Bonnets** when the afternoon watch began.'

'That hot-head! It would be him! Pray heaven, he doesna make things worse. But we must get away, all of us, before that fiend kens what we're doing. Ye must be brave lass noo. We're going to have to go up instead of down. Dick'll let us over the battlements.'

Kirsty nodded again. Her heart was beat-ing wildly. She realized they must escape as quickly as possible. Nebless Nick would kill every one of them if he learnt they'd thwarted him, and as his men were in control of the Tower nobody could do any-thing. So she sat quite still while Elspeth hurriedly dressed her in the warm riding clothes she hadn't worn for such a long time.

'Noo, I'll fetch Dick,' said her nurse and went upstairs. Kirsty crawled to her bed and took from under the pillow the book Francis's mother had sent her, and tucked it into the front of her clothes. Brother John

127

would want her to have it with her. Then Elspeth and Dick came in, arguing together in low tones.

'Use your brains,' Elspeth was imploring. 'Ye ken the Laird'd want the bairn saved before aught else. Keep your temper, lad. Vengence'll do later.'

'Ay, ye'll be reet,' Dick grunted, 'let's see to the guid father first.' Producing a leather bottle he went over to Brother John and managed to get him to drink some of the contents. As the spirits took effect, he helped the monk to his feet. 'Come on noo. Let Elspeth have your arm, your reverence. I'll tak' Mistress Kirsty.'

With immense relief Kirsty allowed herself to be picked up. At last they had somebody to take care of them! And how strong Dick was — he carried Kirsty up to the battlements as easily as if she'd been a baby. Elspeth and the monk followed. The former laiden with several cloaks.

'Not a sound mind,' warned Elspeth as she wrapped one of them round Kirsty, 'Dick's going to let us all down in turn.'

'Ay, an' Elspeth first for she's the fittest o' ye.' said Dick who was busy with a coil of rope.

'You can't do that, Elspeth!' gasped Kirsty suddenly realizing what they were

128

about to attempt, 'you can't go over the battlements! You'll be killed!'

'Hoots, Mistress Kirsty! D'ye think it's the first time I've escaped this way? Keep a guid heart bairn, and pray to the Blessed Virgin nobody sees us.'

And with that Elspeth calmly let Dick fold the other cloak round her and assist her over the parapet. Kirsty lay shivering with fear, her mouth pressed against her wrappings to stop her crying out, and trying desperately to remember her prayers.

'It's a' reet noo,' she heard Dick say, 'she's safe doon. Let's hae ye next, reverend father.'

Brother John seemed to be still dazed from his ordeal for he made no protest as Dick tied him up in a similar fashion and sent him on his way.

It took a little longer, for Dick had to lower him more carefully, but at last he reported: 'He's doon. She's lowsing him. They're baith safe. Hae a keek, Mistress Kirsty. She's waving noo!'

But Kirsty wouldn't venture to peep. She kept her eyes firmly closed as she felt Dick tying her tightly in a bundle. Then she found herself falling gently through space and before she had time to be more frightened, Elspeth's loving arms were round her, lowering her tenderly to the ground.

Kirsty drew a deep breath and poking her head out of her coverings, was just in time to see Dick with bow and spear slung on his back, scramble over the battlements and slide swiftly down the rope.

As he landed beside them he glanced cautiously round, but nobody was about. So signing to the others to follow, he picked Kirsty up and ran to a little postern gate in the outer wall. It opened easily and he carried Kirsty to a clump of bushes where she was out of sight of the Tower. Then he ran back to help Elspeth with Brother John who was still very shaky. Together they helped the monk over to where Kirsty lay and urging the others to follow as quickly as they could Dick once more picked up Kirsty and set off briskly towards the head of the glen.

Now that they were safely beyond the walls Kirsty began to enjoy the adventure. It was so marvellous to be out of doors again. To smell the sweet clean air and hear the birds calling. To see the clouds floating high in the blue sky and feel the soft breeze on her face. It made her almost forget the danger they were in. And she could walk again. What a glorious thought! She would be able to play on the hills once more — or

130

had she just imagined she stood? She must try again as soon as they reached whatever shelter Dick was taking them to.

She was abruptly brought out of her pleasant day dreams when Dick suddenly stopped and swore.

'What is it? What's the matter?' she asked fearfully.

'Wheesht, Mistress Kirsty. Dinna be feart. They've found us gone an' he's sent his sleuth dog after us. Hark!'

Kirsty listened and sure enough far down the glen in the direction of the Tower, she could hear the baying of a great hound. For a minute she had a mental vision of a huge slavering beast tearing her out of Dick's arms, and then she remembered Elspeth and Brother John following behind.

'The others? It'll get them!'

She twisted round so that she could see the two plodding figures, and at the same time Dick moved her to get his right arm free.

'It's a' reet,' Dick said comfortingly, as he pointed and gesticulated, 'Elspeth kens what we've tae do. She's a brave one, that. Noo tae the burn, Mistress Kirsty. We maun gan alang the water tae deaden the scent.'

He strode purposefully to the Biglynn

Burn and then she heard his heavy feet crunching on stones as he waded along it.

They were slower now, for Dick had to watch his footing among the slippery boulders in the bed of the stream. Several times Kirsty thought he was going to drop her as he stumbled but he always righted himself and they went on.

At last the air was filled with the sound of falling water. They were nearly back at the Lynn Pool where all her adventures had begun on that far off day when they rescued Francis.

'Where are we going?' she inquired as he scrambled out of the stream and set her down on the bank.

'To hide in the cave,' said Dick, 'we'll be safe there.'

'We can't. It's too small for us.' objected Kirsty.

'Losh, I'm no meaning the yin ye play in. A' the bairns round aboot ken that.' Dick gave a little laugh, 'There's a real cave ahint the falls, the secret place we keep for refuge. Bide still a while till I fetch the others. They're havin' a sair struggle wi' Elspeth's wet skirts an' the priest's robes.'

Her two friends were indeed in a mess and Brother John looked quite ill, but, again carrying Kirsty Dick hurried them towards the foot of the waterfall. There he picked his way over the boulders at the edge of the Burn and pushing aside a screen of drooping branches, crept into a little opening in the rocks behind the curtain of water.

It was the entrance to a cave the size of a small room. Kirsty looked about her in wonder. She had never dreamt of there being such a place. As well as a faint light from the opening through which they had come, it was lit by a crack in the roof, that Dick said would act as a smoke hole. Only they must wait to make a fire till after dark in case anyone noticed.

There was also a pile of nice dry kindling ready to be lit, and in one corner a heap of springy heather was laid so as to form a bed.

Dick laid Kirsty on it and Elspeth made her comfortable with a cloak round her. Then she told Dick to bring out his leather bottle again.

'Here, drink this, bairn,' she ordered, holding it to Kirsty's lips.

It was horrible. Kirsty felt as if it were burning her mouth and throat. Coughing and spluttering she tried to refuse, but Elspeth insisted.

''Twill warm you and make you sleep,' she said firmly, when she judged Kirsty had enough, 'Stay quiet now while I see what we can do for puir Brother John. He's a worse case than you are.'

So Kirsty lay watching drowsily as Dick and Elspeth removed the monk's robes and chafed his hands and feet. He had slid to the floor as soon as they came into the cave and seemed deeply unconscious again. Would he be alright? She tried to keep her attention on what was happening, but it was no use. In spite of her anxiety her eyes just wouldn't keep open, so finally she closed them altogether and fell fast asleep.

She was aroused, reluctantly, some hours later by the sound of voices, and looking up saw to her surprise that the cave was full of light — and people!

A bright fire was blazing in the stone hearth and Elspeth crouched beside it, stirring something in an iron pot. Brother John cosily wrapped in a cloak like herself, lay nearby. Beyond them Dick was talking earnestly with a shabby old man muffled in a grey plaid.

Kirsty must have made some sound for the stranger suddenly broke off and came towards her. As he did so she saw he was wearing a sword half hidden by his tattered garments. She was just about to scream when she changed to a cry of recognition.

'ANDREW! Oh, dear Andrew! I didn't

134

know you! What are you doing here?'

'Nay, I'd think ye wouldna — in this guise! But I had to come poorly clad lest ony o' the black villain's lot spotted me. Eeh, Mistress Kirsty, we nane o' us kenned what he was at till we got the message fra Elspeth. Pretending 'twas just a neighbourly call, huh! Ye have been a brave wee lass — an' ye'll no mind bidin' here a while — till we get things sorted out an' the Laird comes tae his ain again? I've brought a heap o' supplies, an' another man tae guard ye forby. Here, lad ...'

At his words a small figure who had been squatting by the fire behind Elspeth, rose to its feet and came towards them. It was Sim! He moved slowly and seemed almost shy.

'Mistress Kirsty! Ye — ye saved my life. I — I dinna ken how tae thank ye.' He clumsily grabbed her hand and kissed it, 'I —I'll shed my heart's blood for ye if needs be.'

Kirsty snatched her hand away, remembering Francis's insincere court manners and how easily she had been deceived by them.

'Oh, Sim I'm so glad you're safe — but don't be silly! Oh don't. Sim, something wonderful's happened. I can walk! I'll show you — but — but not now. I'm too tired.'

The acrid smoke was making her eyes sting and she just longed to close them. 'Is — is Brother John all right?' she asked making a last effort.

Dick gave her a wicked grin, his white teeth gleaming as he tried to fix a rushlight in a cleft of the wall.

'That's gied ye a glim! Ay, he's doing fine, Mistress Kirsty. He's had a drap o' the same physic as ye, an' he'll no wake till morn.'

'Oh, that — that's good,' Kirsty let herself relax, 'I—I'm so glad ...'

Her heavy eyelids closed and she drifted off to sleep again. Sim watched her for a few minutes and then resumed his place by the fire.

With his chin on his hands he sat gazing at the dancing flames and thinking of the sad changes the day had brought. His own narrow, oh so narrow escape from Nebless Nick's revenge; his family who had had to flee their simple home because of him and hide in a bothy among the hills. Actually he wasn't so worried about them, for Andrew would see they got some supplies, and his mother was a hill-bred woman who could make one dish of oatmeal go as far as two, forby knowing how to set snares as well as any man. But his beloved master shut away

136

in prison — and Kirsty driven from her rightful place. What did it matter that she could walk again — always supposing she really could — if she had lost her father and her home. He knew her so well and what her state of mind would be if the Laird never returned. And she couldn't live in the cave for ever — what about when winter came? What were they all going to do?

## THE EDINBURGH ROAD

Next time Kirsty woke the cave was dark again for it was full day and they had had to douse the fire. But Dick had been out with his bow at dawn and a savoury stew of rabbit and moor-fowl was keeping warm in the embers.

Sim was at Kirsty's bedside as soon as she stirred. She greeted him with a glad smile, then looked toward the place where Brother John had lain the night before. He wasn't there!

'Dinna fret. He's aw' reet,' said Sim correctly interpreting her stricken expression, 'He was better when he woke up, an' said he must get on his way at once. Elspeth told him he wasna fit, didn't ye, Elspeth? But he would gang.'

'I did that,' agreed Elspeth who was busy pouring some of the stew into a basin, 'You've had a sair dunt, I told him, you're never fit for a long journey, your reverence.'

'But where's he gone?' asked Kirsty, 'not back to Melrose?'

'Ay,' said Sim excitedly, 'that's why he

insisted on starting at first light — lest he met wi' ony o' Nebless Nick's folk. He said if he could only win safe tae Melrose, the head priest there, the Lord Abbot they call him, has the King's ain ear an' he'll send a message tae Edinbro straight away, an' the Laird'll be righted in no time. Eel, I never thought priests had so much power, did ye? But wouldn't it be grand, Kirsty?'

'Oh, it would!' said Kirsty with great relief as she ate a good helping of the stew, and then let Elspeth wash and tidy her. 'But I do just wish I could have told Brother John I can walk now, before he went away,' she added wistfully.

'Oh, but he knew.' Sim assured her, 'he heard it all afore he went. He said it was a miracle o' love, whatever that means, an' ye've tae walk a wee bit every day, just a few steps ye ken, so ye dinna get too tired — an' ye've tae let Elspeth rub your leg with neat's foot oil. We'll tell Andrew tae fetch a jar next time he comes.'

After that nothing would do but Kirsty must try out her new skill right away. So with Dick and Elspeth supporting her she managed a few shaky steps. Sim laughed and cheered her on.

'Bravo Kirsty, ye're doing weel! An ither day I'll mark oot a path on the floor so we'll ken how ye gan on — but - but stop noo. Ye've tae tak' it slow ye ken.'

Elspeth told him he was a sensible boy, and Dick who had been awake all night guarding the cave, said he wanted to rest, but Kirsty who was very elated by her performance, next demanded to go out of doors.

Elspeth was extremely doubtful about this. What if anyone saw them? They had a lengthy discussion and in the end she reluctantly consented to Dick carrying Kirsty to a little sheltered hollow by the bank of the stream where she could lie in the sunlight and not be seen by anyone unless they came right up to her. Sim promised he would keep a close look out for strangers and the two children were left alone.

They had plenty to talk about in the previous day's adventures. Sim told how the little servant girl, Mysie, had gone out pretending to gather sticks, and met him just as he was driving some cattle to the Tower for the afternoon milking. When he'd heard what was happening, Sim had left the beasts to their fate — Mysie was too afraid of them to act as a herdswoman — and bolted for the hill. From a hiding place in the heather he'd seen his mother and the little ones set off for the old shepherd's bothy and eventually joined them there. Till at dusk Andrew had come with meal for them and told him he'd be safer in the cave with Kirsty. Nebless Nick's men could easily recognise him but they wouldn't be sure who his family were.

Then Kirsty described how they had descended from the battlements and her feelings when she suddenly found herself hanging in mid-air. Secretly Sim rather envied her this experience and resolved to get Dick to teach **him** how to walk down walls at the earliest opportunity. The one thing Kirsty didn't say much about was her encounter with Nebless Nick and Sim was too kind-hearted to press her, for he knew from Elspeth what an ordeal it had been.

Next they talked about Brother John, wondering how far he had got on his journey and whether it was one to two day's walk to Melrose — neither of them were very sure about distance. And then how long would it take a man on a swift horse to ride from Melrose to Edinburgh?

Kirsty made some wild but hopeful calculations and Sim wisely abstained from reminding her that in his weak state Brother John was most unlikely to reach the monastery at all.

Presently the warmth of the sun and maybe relief from yesterday's strain — or possibly the last effects of the leather bottle, made Kirsty's head gently nod. Her eyelids drooped and she was sound asleep once more.

Sim sat watching her for a few minutes. She looked very peaceful. Her lips were parted in a half smile and he fancied he could already see the flush of recovered health on her cheeks. It must be the fresh air.

Sim got slowly to his feet. He too would be asleep soon if he wasn't careful. He had had an uneasy night and still felt slightly stiff from lying on the hard floor of the cave. He would just go down the burnside a short way and see if there was any chance of some fishing.

He forced himself to step out briskly, and then suddenly stopped abruptly as he heard a sound which made his blood freeze. It was the same he'd listened to yesterday when he crouched hiding on the hillside. The fearsome baying of a great hound!

Nebless Nick didn't give up as easily as they'd hoped. He must be hunting them again.

Sim looked round frantically, wondering what to do first. It was no good waking Kirsty till he'd found out exactly what was happening. A convenient tree caught his eye and forgetting his aches and pains he scrambled up it. At the second fork he paused, shaded his gaze from the sun and peered down the valley.

Far off he could see a small group of men following a large brown animal that was zig-zagging to and fro across the heath. Yes, Nebless Nick must be determined to get them. It would only be a matter of time till the sleuth dog found the scent of where the fugitives had entered and left the stream.

Sim hurtled down from the tree and rushed to the cave.

'DICK! DICK!' he cried, shaking the trooper who was sprawled on Kirsty's heather couch, 'Rise an' get get Mistress Kirsty. Quick! He's loosed the dog again.'

'DOG?' Dick was awake on the instant. He was used to sudden alarms. 'Where?'

'Gae tae the back o' the cave, Elspeth,' he went on, placing his spear against a rock at the mouth of the cave where it would be handy, 'I'll fetch the bairn. An' take my dagger — I may no be able tae defend ye long.'

'Ay an' I'll use it too if needs be' said Elspeth accepting the weapon, 'Blessed Saints protect us! I'll no see the bairn mauled by yon brute.'

'If ye could shoot it ...' Sim began, then

143

stopped, knowing it was a silly suggestion. Once let the dog reach the vicinity of the cave and they would soon be discovered. If Nebless Nick had not already heard rumours of such a hiding place, he might torture some of their own folk to gain the information.

'I ken what tae do!' he exclaimed suddenly. Dick had left the cave. 'Give me ane o' ye're petticoats, Elspeth, an' something o' Kirsty's. I'll lead the beast astray — hurry, afore Kirsty comes ben or she'll cry on me to stay.'

Elspeth grasped the idea instantly. She tore off one of her underskirts and thrust it at him, along with Kirsty's cloak.

'Heaven keep ye, lad! Safe oot an' safe in!'

She was bidding him farewell as if he were a grown man about to go on a raid, but Sim was too desperately anxious to feel proud. Gripping the garments in hands already clammy with fear, he brushed past Dick who was returning with Kirsty, and made off as quickly as possible. There was no time now for pleading or arguing.

As Sim went down the valley he had to force himself to move slowly for he knew he would need all his strength for the task ahead — and all his courage too if he was to get the better of Nebless Nick's ferocious hound.

At last the noise of the dog and the men who were urging it on became uncomfortably close. They were also getting very near to the place where Sim judged his friends must have taken to the water the previous day.

Luckily there were plenty of bushes growing here and taking advantage of every bit of cover. Sim crawled about with the clothes Elspeth had given him, dragging behind.

He moved in this way until he had directed the scent away from the stream and over a piece of rising ground and was out of sight of the pursuers. Then still trailing the garments, he took to his heels and ran as he had never done before.

Soon the baying of the dog grew louder, more excited, as it picked up the fresh scent, and Sim tore over the ground with his heart throbbing madly and his breath coming in short painful gasps. He knew where he was making for but his eyes seemed unable to focus and the sweat running down his face made them sting. It was as if there was nothing in the world but himself and the howling monster which was catching up on him every minute.

Then suddenly he felt the grass give beneath his feet and knew he was on swampy ground. He had reached his objective.

Throwing himself down against a tussock, he waited — knife at the ready. The dog now free of its leash, had far out distanced the men, and a few minutes later came bounding into the hollow with blazing eyes and bared teeth. Giving a horrible snarl it leaped straight at Sim but the boy was prepared. Raising his knife he drove it hard into the beast's heart. The creature yelled, rolled over and gave a shuddering groan.

Sim knelt by the body almost sobbing with relief as he withdrew his knife and wiped it clean. He was so utterly weary he would have liked to lie down on the soft sward beside the animal and rest for ever — but the men might come next and he couldn't fight **them.**

He was near the edge of a small peat bog with pools of brackish water among the moss-hags. Making a great effort he dragged the dog's body towards one of them and carefully pushed it in. There was a weird gurgling sound and the corpse sank without a trace.

Far off the men were whistling and hallooing for their lost charge. Sim daren't stay any longer. Summoning all his strength he began running back up the valley, but it was hard going. Then a dreadful thought struck him. What if Nebless Nick had another hound in reserve? It would be wiser to return by the stream. Sim turned to the burnside and stepped into the water.

The coolness felt delicious against his hot, tired feet but he soon found it was imposs-ible to make haste when wading up the slippery bed of a swiftly flowing rivulet.

He struggled on till he was as near to the Lynn Pool as it was safe to go. He scrambl-ed up the bank and thoroughly exhausted, collapsed on the ground like a stone.

He knew nothing more till he heard Dick's voice close by and opened his eyes to find the reiver bending over him.

'Eeh, Sim man, that was a grand race! I've never seen the like! I near fell out o' yon tree wi' the excitement o' it. An' ye slew the beast too I guess. I must get the blood off afore ye meet the women-folk.'

He bathed Sim's face and hands and then picked him up in the way he did with Kirsty. Sim, somewhat annoyed, protested he was neither a baby or a little girl to be carried so but Dick soon silenced him.

'I've heard the Laird say that when a man acts the hero his fellows aye carry him abune them, sae haud ye're wheesht, lad.'

He was next fussed over by Kirsty and Elspeth in the most embarrassing way, and even given the last few drops of fiery spirit from the leather bottle, but Sim was too tired to care about anything. He only wanted to sleep and sleep.

When he woke again — the following day — he found Kirsty full of questions, — and fears. Her nerves were still bad from her long illness and she had taken it into her head that Nebless Nick would soon be hunting them with more dogs.

Happily for everyone Andrew paid them a visit that night and was able to reassure her. Their enemy had left Biglynn Tower he informed them with much satisfaction. Some of their own men had slipped away under cover of darkness and crossing into the next valley had burnt the outbuildings and several haystacks at Nebless Nick's home and the villain was forced to return hot-foot to see what was going on. But he'd left some of his followers with the Biglynn garrison so it would not yet be safe for Elspeth and the children to reveal their presence. Nebless Nick might come back any day.

'So ye must e'en be brave bairns a while longer,' said Andrew in his kindly way, after he'd praised Sim's exploit, 'an' bide contented till we see how things gang.'

Nor should Kirsty worry about her father he went on, for no reiver **ever** stayed in prison if he'd friends to get him out — and the world knew the Laird had plenty of those.

Kirsty was used to her father being absent for lengthy periods so she accepted this and settled to enjoy the strange new life in the cave quite happily. Her health improved rapidly for she spent every possible moment in the open air. Sometimes sailing leaf boats down the stream or merely sitting still with her feet dabbling in the sparkling water.

She also regained the full use of her legs, and much quicker than Sim had dared to hope, his dream of seeing her running about again came true. And what merry days they had playing on the hillside and searching for luscious blaeberries among the heather while faithful Dick kept watch further up the slope ready to give a peewit's warning cry at the sight of any stranger.

So the days and weeks sped by, and there was still no news of Big Wat. At length Sim got a definite impression something was wrong. Elspeth was becoming slightly short tempered and even Dick wasn't as cheery as usual, and once or twice had caught the grown-ups whispering together when Kirsty was out of the way.

His little friend must have sensed it too.

'Sim, don't you think Father **ought** to be coming back soon?' she asked suddenly one day, 'don't you think he'll have escaped by now? We've been in the cave MONTHS — and — I — I'm getting frightened for him!'

Sim tried to soothe her with a reminder of Andrew's words and pointed out that Edinburgh was a very long way off. Anything could have delayed the Laird.

Kirsty fell silent then. Sim was hoping he'd put her mind at rest when the business of the surprise gave their thoughts a completely new turn.

It began when Andrew in his shepherd disguise, came earlier than usual and caught Kirsty watching the many coloured sunset clouds which were piling up in the west.

'Losh, Mistress Kirsty, 'he said looking closely at her, 'I hadna realised ye were growing into such a bonny lass.' It was the first time he'd seen her in true daylight since she became ill. 'But what a tatterdemalion! I must mind an' fetch ye a decent dress.'

Kirsty laughed cheekily at him. One of the good things about living in the cave was that Elspeth couldn't fuss over torn clothes. But when he did bring her the dress she opened the parcel with a cry of dismay.

'Oh Andrew, this is my best blue one! It should have been the russet. I can't wear this here.'

'Weel ye couldna expect me tae ken aught aboot women's clothes,' Andrew replied teasingly, 'but next time I come — that'll be twa days hence I'm thinking — let's see ye garbed like a young lady for a change. 'Twill remind us o' the guid auld times — an' maybe I'll hae a surprise for ye.'

This was quite enough to make Kirsty forget about the dress, and all next day the children puzzled and argued as to what the surprise might be.

Neither of them were used to unexpected treats and they were all agog to know what it could be. Sim being most practical, thought it would be something to eat, honeycomb perhaps or a piece of venison. Kirsty swayed between a kitten and some ribbons to match her dress. Then deciding Elspeth must be in on the secret, she pestered so much, her nurse said in exasperation, she hoped it would be a whip. While Dick suggested a scold's bridle, a metal gag for punishing quarrelsome women, would be more suitable.

Kirsty was so angry at this she paid Dick out by throwing his helmet into the pool and wouldn't say she was sorry. Elspeth sent her to bed without any supper but Kirsty's naughty mood only lasted till everyone else was asleep. Lying awake in the dark she felt truly grieved for the way she'd treated Dick — who'd been so good to them — and said a little prayer for forgiveness as Brother John had taught her. Afterwards she was much happier and fell asleep resolving to apologise to Dick first thing in the morning.

But when she woke in the grey light of dawn it was the surprise which was foremost in her mind. She was sure she knew the solution.

Getting up quickly and quietly she tiptoed over to Sim and in a whisper urged him to follow her outside.

'Och Kirsty, can ye no let a man get his sleep out?' he grumbled, ''tis a raw damp morn. Ye canna gang on the hill this early.'

'I must.' said Kirsty firmly, 'Sim, I know what the surprise is! FATHER MUST BE COMING HOME! — and that's why ...'

'Andrew wanted ye tae wear your best dress. Of course.'

'We must go and meet him.' Kirsty went on eagerly, 'Now, at once before they wake up. Oh, isn't it splendid! I can't wait to show him how I can walk. He'll be so pleased.'

'We've had naught tae eat yet,' Sim objected, an' we dinna ken which way he's comin'.'

'OH Sim, don't be stupid! You know he's in Edinburgh so he'll come back by the Edinburgh road of course. We must just go along the valley till we reach it. We won't be long — and Father will bring us back quickly on the horses. We'll all eat then. Elspeth will have the porridge ready.'

'But — but suppose we fall in with Nebless Nick's lot?' Sim was fighting a loosing battle and knew it.

'They'll not bother us now,' Kirsty was quite confident, 'not when Father's here with a plump of spears (troop of spearmen) at his back. Just think, Sim, he'll beat Nebless Nick and we'll be able to go home properly.'

It was no use. Kirsty's enthusiasm was catching and Sim gave way. So they set off briskly into the morning mist just as the sun came peeping over the furtherest edge of the hills.

After they'd gone a couple of miles Kirsty's legs began to drag sooner than they'd have done before she was ill. Her inside felt rather hollow too, but it had been her idea to come so she kept bravely, only stopping to look at a flower or pick an invisible berry with increasing frequency. Anything for a minute's rest.

At last they scrambled over a crest of the moorland and there was the Edinburgh road, a broad track worn by the passing of armies over the years, winding away before them — but as far as they could see there wasn't a living thing on it.

Tears sprang to Kirsty's eyes, She'd let her imagination run away with her again and fully expected that when they reached the road they'd see Big Wat riding towards them. It was such a disappointment!

'My legs ache,' she said sitting down, 'and I'm so tired. Oh, I wish we'd waited to have breakfast first.'

'Ay, I telt ye we should.' Sim replied dourly.

'I know, you're right,' admitted Kirsty, 'but if we had Elspeth wouldn't have let us come and I do want to see Father again.' She gave a little sob.

'Look,' said Sim, 'I think there's a cot-house over there. I saw smoke afore. Let's go an' see if they'll give us aught tae eat.'

'Oh yes. Do. What a good idea.'

They turned away from the road and went towards a fold in the hills.

'You wait here,' ordered Sim when they came in sight of the little house,' behind yon bushes till I see what sort of folk they are.'

Kirsty gratefully settled herself in the lee of the bushes and must have nodded off, for it didn't seem long before Sim was back with some stale oatcakes which were all he'd managed to persuade the cottage woman to give him.

They shared them out and Sim hoped Kirsty would now think about returning home.

'Oh not just yet,' she said when he suggested it, 'I want to go back to the road and wait just a little longer. Please Sim. Father might come yet — it's still early.'

Sim sighed. Well, let her have another look at the road and then he ought to insist on going back. Dick and Elspeth must already be anxious about them, and he rather thought he'd heard thunder.

They trudged to their former position over the rise above the road — then stopped and gasped in amazement.

The wide grassy track was no longer empty. A vast column of men and horses which seemed to stretch almost to the horizon were coming along it.

There were plumed knights and banners fluttering; footmen, archers, baggage wagons and led pack-horses.

Never had the children seen anything like

it before. They stood in stunned silence as the great procession lumbered towards them, preceeded by a company of well-armed horsemen.

Sim came to himself first. 'Lie doon, Kirsty!' he gasped, 'We maunna let them see us. It's no the Laird — he'd never have a troop that size. They're maybe English invadin' us.'

He spoke too late. They had been spotted. Somebody shouted an order and two riders instantly came spurring up the hillside.

The children turned and ran. But it was no use, in a few minutes the men caught up with them. As they sprang from their horses Sim drew his knife and stepped in front of Kirsty.

The first man laughed. 'Put up your dagger, young gamecock,' he said quite kindly, and to the children's relief, in the Scots tongue, 'an' tell us that ye do here, spying on the King's army?'

Kirsty didn't know what he meant but she suddenly remembered that in spite of her rags, she was a Laird's daughter, and spoke out firmly.

I'm looking for my father. Big Wat Elliot. He's coming from Edinburgh. Have you seen him?'

The men glanced at each other, then the first one peered rather suspiciously at Kirsty.

'Big Wat? He's ahint there. We heard them say he'd a bairn he was wantin' back to — but I thought she was a cripple.'

'Oh yes, but I'm better now. Look, that's where I was shot.' Kirsty lifted her skirt to show the scar on her leg, in a way which would have horrified Elspeth, 'Oh, take me to Father. Quickly, please.'

She treated the man to her most appealing smile, and he immediately lifted her to his saddle, saying to his companion, 'You take the boy' as he did so.

They trotted back along the side of the moving column, pausing every now and then to enquire where Big Wat might be.

Sim tried to take in details of all the fine weapons and armour he was seeing, but Kirsty looked only for her father.

Then at last she saw him, surrounded by a group of the most magnificent knights, but still wearing the old rusty armour he'd ridden away in and mounted on his favourite horse, Black Roger.

'FATHER!' shrieked Kirsty, and almost fell out of her new friend's arms as he passed her over to Big Wat like some struggling animal.

The horsemen nearby all stopped and drew aside from the procession to watch the reunion. Kirsty took no notice of them. She just clung to her father and rained kisses on his face as she sobbed out the story of her adventures. As she told about Nebless Nick there were many loud expressions of anger from the company.

'Struck the holy priest, did he! God curse him! We never heard that bit o' the tale before!'

'Is he all right? Brother John?' asked Kirsty tremulously, 'Is he here too?'

'Safe an' well, my doo, an' praise the Blessed Virgin for it! 'Twas thanks tae him my name was cleared. We wanted him tae come along wi' us but he wouldna. He said a royal progress was no place for him.'

'Royal?' Kirsty only half understood, 'Father, d'you mean…?'

'Ay,' the grand knight next to Big Wat broke in — he used the same broad Border dialect as the men — 'the King's come tae our marches tae see justice is done. An' ye need never fear Nick Armstrong mair. He'll no trouble ye again. He was blown out yestermorn.'

'B-blown?' Kirsty lifted her tear-wet face and stared at him.

'Lord Maxwell is telling you Nebless

Nick's been outlawed,' her father explained with a smile, 'by proclamation and sound of bugle — declared beyond the law for giving false evidence against me. He must leave the country noo. Biglynn's a' oor ain again — an' Brother John'll be waiting there for us — but we must attend on the King before we can gang hame.'

'That we must.' Lord Maxwell joined in once more, 'If His Grace is to sup in my castle at Lochmaben I must speed there tae welcome him. An' if Lady Christine's to be presented she'll need a tirewoman (dresser) in attendance. Here Lance,' he beckoned the man who'd brought Kirsty, 'take the boy to guide ye, an' get the old nurse, an' that dress — oh, an' a spare horse for the jackman too. His loyalty deserves reward. Noo Wat man, hold fast to your treasure an' let's awa'. We've to reach Lochmaben long ere sunset.'

At that the men under Lord Maxwell's personal command turned rapidly away from the slower moving main column and struck off across the hills in a breakneck gallop. Kirsty cuddled in the safety of her father's arm and wrapped in a cloak someone had lent for her, continued chattering as best she could. Big Wat answered at random. Could Mysie have a new dress? ...

160

or would a silver coin be better? ... and what about a helmet for Dick? ... Yes, of course ... and Sim? Oh, certainly something must be done for Sim.

Kirsty had everything planned out — to her own satisfaction at least — when they finally drew rein in the courtyard of a noble castle standing on the banks of a beautiful lake.

There strange servants looked after her till Elspeth arrived, an Elspeth so excited she laughed and scolded in the same breath as she bathed Kirsty in a large tub of hot, sweet scented water before a roaring log fire.

Just as they finished several lovely ladies wearing gorgeous silks and satins, entered the room. They fussed and cooed over Kirsty, praising her looks and courage in such exaggerated fashion Elspeth sniffed with disapproval.

Kirsty didn't know what to say, so she merely listened quietly as Elspeth told her to be on her best behaviour — especially if the King was near — and mind her table manners. At the same time she tied Kirsty's hair with a gold ribbon one of the ladies gave her and put on her best dress, which now alas, didn't look anything special.

A few minutes later Kirsty forgot about

her clothes, for the prettiest of the ladies led her to a huge room, far bigger than the great hall at home, all decorated with pennons, banners, and branches of evergreens.

It was full of people milling about everywhere. Kirsty felt quite lost till suddenly through the throng, she caught a glimpse of Dick drinking wine among the crowd of men and obviously enjoying himself very much.

Then the lady nudged Kirsty gently and bid her curtsy to the King's Grace and kiss his hand. Kirsty had a brief impression of a fine gentleman with curly hair and an auburn beard, wearing a jewelled collar and a suit of rich velvet, before she lowered her eyes and tried to concentrate on her curtsy. It was a terrible moment. **Both** her legs seemed like jelly and she was sure the injured one would give way. But with great effort she managed to raise herself and timidly kissed the slender hand extended towards her. She was too shy to look up again, but she could feel someone patting her head, and a musical masculine voice said: 'A winsome little lass, and I'm told as brave as she's bonny. You must be proud of her, Wat Elliot!'

The lady took Kirsty's hand again and led her away, saying over her shoulder, 'Go take your pleasure, Wat. I'll look after her.'

She guided Kirsty to a seat at a long table between herself and another gentleman, and signed to a servant to bring some watered wine and a platter of roast meat for the little girl.

Kirsty could hardly eat at first for she was so fascinated by everything around her. It seemed as if the meal were going to last all night for there was an endless variety of dishes. Loins of beef, haunches of venison, sides of mutton, hares, rabbits and birds of every kind, not to mention numerous lesser dishes of which she couldn't even guess the ingredients, but were so enticing it was difficult to choose between them.

Kirsty couldn't see the King or her father but presently she managed to spot Sim further down the table. He was very smart in a bright green tunic. Kirsty tried to catch his eye, but every time she looked he seemed to be lifting something to his mouth. Poor Sim, they'd so often played at imaginary feasts she couldn't blame him for making the most of a real one when he'd the chance — and with that Kirsty put out her own hand and took another little cake made of honey and almonds from a dish beside her. They really were delicious. She wondered if kings ate like this **every** day.

Just then in came the royal jester, very

gay in a costume of red and yellow, and a cap hung with little bells which jangled as he moved. He reminded Kirsty of the show-man with the animals, but instead of four-legged creatures this man had two grot-esque dwarfs who pranced about among the half-empty dishes on the table, while their master ran along side cracking jokes Kirsty didn't understand but which brought roars of laughter from the company.

The noise, the heat from the torches on the walls, and the smell of food was almost overpowering. Kirsty actually found herself quite thankful when the lovely lady whisper-ed, 'Time for bed. Your father'll come up to you later.'

Kirsty had settled down between clean soft sheets in the bed she was to share with Elspeth, when Big Wat arrived, dressed like a courtier as he'd been when they were presented to the King.

'Comfortable, Elspeth?' he asked looking about him.

"Deed I am, Laird,' said Elspeth busy tidying Kirsty's clothes, ''Tis like heaven after those weeks in the cave.'

Big Wat came over and sat by Kirsty.

'Was — was my curtsy all right, Father? she asked anxiously. It was the only thing that worried her. She was convinced she'd wobbled and what would her father say if she'd disgraced him before all those people?

'It was perfect,' Big Wat assured her, 'ye couldna hae done better, my doo. His Grace was charmed wi' ye. An' what d'ye think, he's gi'en me a' Nebless Nick's land tae hold in trust till ye are woman grown an' ready tae be a great lady at court.'

'Oh, but I don't want to be a grand lady — not now or ever. It's been wonderful tonight — like a fairy tale. But what I really want is just to stay at home with you, and Elspeth, and Sim, and all our people.'

'Um,' said Big Wat in a teasing voice, 'it's a very serious thing to refuse a king's gift. Would it be best if I ask His Grace tae gie it tae Sim so he can become a knight an' wed the lady o' his choice?'

'Yes,' said Kirsty sleepily as she snuggled down into the feather mattress. It was like lying on a cloud she thought. 'That — would — be different. Oh Father, won't we be very happy tomorrow? I can't wait to go home.'

## THE END

## AUTHOR'S NOTE

You will search in vain to find Biglynn Glen on any map. I imagine it to be somewhere near Eskdale in the former county of Dumfriesshire, the area which was known in the 16th Century as the Western Marches of Scotland.

But if you are ever lucky enough to travel through the lovely Border country you'll see the hills where the beacons used to blaze and notice the remains of many little pele towers like the one Kirsty lived in — though they don't all have oubliettes in the basement!

Even more exciting, you might be able to see a hound trail and watch the animals which are said to be descended from the sleuth dogs that tracked the raiders, racing over the moorland along the line of a previously laid aniseed scent. Or you may attend one of the annual Common Ridings, the Border's own special festivals, when crowds assemble with bands and banners to remember the wild raiding days, and watch the young folk of the district ride out in the steps of their ancestors, up steep slopes and through rushing rivers with the same reckless courage for which the people of the Brave Borderland have always been renowned.

M.A. Wood is a writer and lecturer who lives near Carlisle. Her other historical novels for children are **The Year the Raiders Came** (also available from Byway Books) which features several of the same characters as this story, and **Master Deor's Apprentice.**